BURNOUT

BURNOUT

BURNOUT

SEAN PLATT
JOHNNY B. TRUANT

STERLING & STONE

Chapter One

JASON RUIZ HAD NEVER SEEN a ghost before.

Not in the building, not in the lobby, not at any of the markets. Not in his closet as a kid and certainly never inside the vault where he usually worked alone — except perhaps the few times executives had borrowed the space; who knew what they did once the doors were closed.

Sure, you heard about ghosts, and everyone claimed they'd rubbed shoulders with one — even done business at an off-regs market. But such stories were typically bullshit. People liked to talk about walking society's edge, but few really did it.

Deal with ghosts, and you might become one.

Promenade talked as if you could catch a way of life like a cold — and something that, if not for the work of sweepers, would rip through good cities like a plague. Rumor claimed that people who spent too much time around ghosts became anonymous by proximity: a contact high that stripped their data and left them blank. People like that, it was said, could simply vanish one day without even knowing they were gone.

They'd wander until a sweep brought them in or put them down. Even friends and family wouldn't come to claim them.

"You won't have to do anything," the executive told Jason as they watched the ghost through the glass. "Just sit there and pretend you're an executive. Or better yet, stand by the door with your arms crossed. Try to look intimidating."

The request was as strange and secretive as the rest of this, but the executive's bearing made him reluctant to argue. She'd introduced herself as Nicola and wore a suit fine enough to class her ten or more rungs above Jason — enough that he felt an absurd impulse to avert his eyes.

Her partner had been large, like Jason, and not as well-dressed as his coworker. The ghost had, Jason suspected, liberated one or more of the man's testicles when he'd kicked him with the glass toe melted to the tip of his boot. The ambulance came quickly to the more trafficked main building, but a replacement executive had not. That put Jason on the button — and now here he was in a clerk's jumper, preparing to enter a sacred space where he didn't belong.

He shouldn't ask what was about to happen or how he was going to pass as an executive without a change of clothing. "How do I look intimidating?"

"Be large. Don't smile." She reached for his face. "Maybe lose the glasses. Tough guys don't wear glasses."

Jason liked the part about standing by the door. Let the lady take the brunt of the man's low validity. Let *her* risk erasure. He had no dog in … whatever this was. His usually quiet job as a clerk was a paycheck. He and Hollander Sitwell had a simple agreement: he filed whatever needed to be filed for eight hours a day, never looking at the documents and obeying only the small paper tabs on each one. At the end of every week, his balance increased by six hundred ducats. A meager but solid living, and not one he planned to risk his identity for.

"What if he speaks to me?" Jason asked.

"Ignore him."

"What if he's still got something up his sleeve? What if he comes at me?"

"He won't."

"How do you know?"

"Because I'm the brains," she said, "and you're the muscle."

That didn't really explain anything. It was actually a lot more logical to run at the muscle than the brains, but again, Jason reminded himself not to ask questions. "When this happened before, they sent me out of the room."

"Yeah. Well."

Jason realistically didn't have a choice here. He'd been credentialed by the skin of his immigrant mother's teeth and didn't want to test his status. That meant staying on the right side of things. *No risks*. Hollander Sitwell said *jump*, and it was in Jason's best interest to find out exactly how high he should go.

His eyes went to the ghost inside the filing room, sitting patiently behind the double-wide table where Jason ate lunch and sometimes played poker with the guards after hours. The place wasn't official; not a holding cell even in the loosest of terms. There were no bars or restraints. The door closed on a thumb button — an obsolete lock for an obsolete building, non-biometric and non-digital for obvious reasons — and Jason had a big set of keys he used for a lot of Hollander Sitwell's office work that would lock the outer door.

That was about it. Nobody ever came here (nobody

wanted all this hard-copy, touch-it-with-your-hands crap), so the building barely needed security.

Of course, that's exactly why the executives had come. Because the records office was offline and therefore as invisible as whoever they brought here.

Who kept paper records these days without being compelled by law? Even the auditors only cared about Jason's work when the government required it.

The glass was not one-way. So as they watched the ghost, the ghost watched them. He looked so cool and unconcerned, considering the damage he'd done and the trouble he'd caused.

"Stay behind me, and you'll be fine," said the executive.

The smell of soil permeated his nostrils as they entered. He'd heard they were people of the earth, so apparently, they rolled around in it. It wasn't an unpleasant smell. It reminded him of Abuela's garden — not that he'd ever admit it, seeing as Abuela, if she'd still been alive, might well have been a ghost herself.

"So this is how it ends. Sitwell's so hard up, I get the bottom of the barrel to interrogate me." The ghost gave him a nod.

Nicola glanced back at Jason. "He's junior to the man whose balls you kicked open, but rest assured he's not 'bottom of the barrel.'"

"I meant you," said the ghost.

Nicola didn't acknowledge him. Jason saw the slightest lift of one eyebrow, but otherwise, she kept her gaze on the tablet, presumably reviewing his case.

The man looked right at Jason.

He was different than expected, though Jason could not have said why. His dust-scuffed black boots and jeans were so crusted with dirt that it'd become structural. He wore a simple white shirt beneath a long flapping duster. Cash-carrying, from-the-gutters, disconnected and entirely off the books. *Like rats,* said the Promenade. The kind of people tolerated because the world needed bodies for the mill and someone to scrub its toilets.

His stare was hard. Unblinking.

Nicola finally sat opposite him and situated her tablet. Only after ten long seconds did the ghost turn his gaze from Jason to her.

When the executive finally looked up, she was clearly concealing her surprise and failing to come off as cool as she must have wanted to. "Your name is Cutter Dunn."

"Sure it is. Do I get a prize?"

"*The* Cutter Dunn?"

"Oh, fun. I'm famous."

"Answer the question."

"Or what? You'll have me arrested?"

When Nicola didn't remotely react, the ghost — *Cutter,* apparently — showed what struck Jason as his first real beat of fear.

"Not *arrested*, then," Cutter said.

"Do you know where you are?"

Cutter shook his head. "I was escorted here kindly and in great style … with a bag over my head."

"This is the paper records annex on the headquarters campus."

"I'm not good enough for the holding facility up at the main building?"

"They're still making sure all the little goodies you planted are found and removed before anyone re-occupies main. Half the lights are burned out. Sorry: *blown* out. There's glass everywhere, of course. Nobody wants blood tracked all over, either."

Nicola crossed her legs. "But that's not the main reason

we're here. Figured you'd be at home in a place like this, with all the paper and light switches. It's a dead spot on the IOT grid. Not even connected to facility power. The building runs off a generator. It's the only place on company property that doesn't exist in any way that matters. A nonexistent place for a nonexistent man." She leaned back. "Tell me. How have *you* stayed so invisible?"

"I'd rather not say."

"Maybe my coworker could beat it out of you."

Cutter looked over at Jason, but fortunately not too hard. The only thing Jason could *beat* was a mean beat on a drum kit.

"Threatening me. Openly."

Nicola shrugged. "You're off the census, from what I can tell. You've breached a private facility on private land, aggressively and destructively, so I figure we can deal with you however we'd like. You're nobody, Dunn — not even after putting modern trucking on the map. Even after years of gainful employment, not even the taxman knows your name."

"But you do."

"You used to have a real 'company man' reputation around here, Dunn. I want to know how you got inside our facility and how you've gotten halfway across the country unseen, but most of all, I want to know what happened to the integrity this company seems to think you have. You get more props from the engineers around here than either Hollander *or* Sitwell. V-See wouldn't exist without you, and now here you are, trying to undo it all. You were compensated well for your work at HS. It's my understanding that you were even given a generous settlement upon leaving."

"You mean my hush money?"

"I mean your settlement. Gainful employment is hard enough these days, *especially* for a ghost. Yet, somehow you managed to get not just a salary for years but also an extra shitload of ducats on your way out the door. I'd think you'd be grateful."

"Let me ask you a question. Are you federal?"

"I'm with HS. Like I said, this is a private matter."

"If you were federal, I might be able to explain to you why nothing they gave me matters. Or, hey. Maybe Big Stuff over there could explain it for me."

They both turned to Jason, who was expecting literally anything else. After a few seconds, it became clear the executive wanted him to speak.

"Who, me?" Jason asked.

"I worked the line at the Jennings plant before I got into V-See," Cutter said, nodding to Jason. "I know what a clerk's jumper looks like. So why don't *you* tell her, chubs? You file the papers, so you must know all about it."

"I don't look at the files," Jason told him.

"Of course not. They're confidential. But you can tell her *why* the records are kept on paper, right? Go on. Tell the nice lady about Conditional Income."

Jason could only stammer, so Cutter explained for him.

"After Hollander Sitwell got into AI, especially with the trucks, doing business in dollars started to cost the company a fortune. Too many micro-transactions and too many business units trying to pretend they were unrelated to avoid antitrust laws. The commissions and transaction fees were killing them. Ducats, as currency, started with Hollander Sitwell's lobbyists. Bet you didn't know that. Trivia's fun, right?"

"Your point?"

Cutter was still staring at Jason. "I queued you up. You do the rest."

Again Nicola looked back. Jason stammered again and

said, "I guess …" He tried again. "I guess people didn't like the idea of digital money without some sort of proof showing who had how much of it. You can't hold ducats in your hand, and a lot of people said it was like paying with air. You have to trust a currency if you're going to use it. After what happened with Bitcoin … "

"I know about Bitcoin!" Nicola snapped.

"Well, Congress didn't want that to happen again. So, in addition to all the tech requirements to stay in compliance, minters of ducats have to keep detailed records of how much of it goes where. *Paper* records because paper can't be hacked."

"And?" the executive asked Cutter.

"My severance pay was issued between government audits. The paper documenting that compensation — proof that I actually own the ducats that blipped into my account and then out again — just … disappeared."

"There must be multiple copies," said the executive.

"Usually, yes. As I understand it, most ducats are documented in a few places, quadruple-checked, and backed up with digital records, just to be sure. That's for *legitimate* transactions. There are a lot fewer copies for less serious transactions. Maybe just one copy. Wouldn't want under-the-table pay to be fact-checked too thoroughly by the IRS, am I right? But I guess that's the downside of being someone like me. The company always had to pay me under the table, with the catch being that it could disappear at any time. Take my money and skim everyone else's, then stuff the right pockets and keep your footprint in the shadows; *that's* how Hollander rolls. But hey. It's all just business, baby."

"Are you're claiming the company rigged the system? That they're skimming funds and—"

"Well, yes. *Fraud, embezzlement, undocumented kickbacks …*

and a lot of off-books, non-credentialed workers paid whenever the company feels like it — folks who end up having no guaranteed income or rights. It's rigged, and a lot of fat cats are getting even fatter on the cream … but that's not even the point right now. Point right now is that I went to withdraw what I had coming to me, and the bank said I was poor as ever."

"Is that what this is about? You wanted to extort the company for money you think you're owed?"

"Money I *am* owed," Cutter replied. "But no. I'm setting the record straight. Consider it a public service."

"If it's not about money, why are you here?"

"You know why."

Understanding passed between the two at the table. Jason, getting none of it, could only wonder.

"Who else was involved?" Nicola asked.

"Nobody."

"Bullshit."

"Nobody," Cutter repeated.

"Were you after the mainframe?"

Cutter shrugged. "Destroy the mainframe, destroy the guidance. Good luck running V-See without a map for the trucks to follow."

"Destroy the …" She half-laughed. "But everything's backed up. A thousand times backed up. Haven't you ever heard of the cloud?"

"What cloud?"

Now the executive laughed, finding herself back on top of the conversation. Cutter got *A's* for effort but *F's* for knowledge. From what Jason was gathering, the commotion up at the main building had been this man's doing, and it'd been bad. He'd managed — somehow — to get through all that security and nearly destroy the mainframe running all the unmanned shipping routes.

From what Jason heard, it had been a near thing. He'd come extremely close to succeeding ... but even *Jason* knew the mainframe's data was backed up. Had been, everywhere, for decades.

But maybe a ghost wouldn't know that. They were off-grid, working with wrenches and gears, shovels and axes. They were also suspicious, believing that every billboard that tried to read their identity and every smart screen's knowledge of their purchase history was akin to stealing their souls.

Cutter looked at his watch (mechanical, of course) and shook it. "What time is it?"

"You're in a lot of trouble here, Mr. Dunn," Nicola said. "I imagine you wanted to make some sort of a statement, breaking into the Hollander Sitwell campus and going after the Big Bad Wolf. But it's a no-fly zone for ten miles in every direction, meaning no news drones saw what you did. Your boom wasn't big enough. If you weren't lying, and you really are working alone, then nobody knows you're here. And that's how it'll stay unless you start talking."

"Is that a threat? *Another* threat?"

"I don't know. What do you think?"

Cutter tapped the table. He leaned back, then forward again.

Jason almost felt bad for the man. Cutter had come here expecting to execute a heist, and now he was trapped in his failure.

Ghosts were powerless at the best of times ... and now, here was one with no options, allies, or means of escape. Jason had no idea why Cutter had done whatever he'd done, but he knew the feeling of being squeezed. Of being on the bottom, without any options.

That's how things had been for Mama and Abuela.

Another few days, and that's how it would have been for Jason, too. A three-day-later postmark and his own papers never would have hit Central in time.

"Fine," Cutter said. "I'll explain. But first, tell me what time it is."

"Why?"

"Sunset. Where I come from, truth comes in daylight, and the lies come at night. Give me a clear conscience, at least."

Nicola, with a suffering sigh, looked down at her watch. "It's seven-fifteen."

"Fifteen more minutes, then." Cutter nodded, taking his time. "Fine. But we do this my way."

"And what way is that?"

"I come from storytellers. I'll give you the long version … or nothing at all."

Chapter Two

"CUTTER," said Dorothy Malko, running up in her homemade dress. It hadn't rained in a few weeks, and the clay beneath the shipping containers had grown a dusty topcoat that swirled in her wake and left a cloud around her ankles. "Thank God. I've been looking everywhere. I thought maybe you'd gone rambling."

Cutter laughed. "You sound like Boots."

Dorothy didn't laugh with him. He didn't ramble; that was the joke. His grandfather had been trying to kick him from the nest his entire life, but Cutter would only ever ramble on a leash. He'd walk away from Amenity with a backpack and his best intentions but always came right back home.

At first, it was for his mother, and after she passed, it was for his mother's father. But Boots would have none of his sympathies. If the cancer hadn't killed him yet, Boots reckoned he'd live forever.

Watching Dorothy's face now, Cutter suspected that was no longer true.

"It's happening, isn't it? It's time."

SEAN PLATT & JOHNNY B. TRUANT

She'd cry when he died, of course; *everyone* cried when there was a funeral in Amenity. The ad-hoc settlement had grown large enough to have roads, a doctor, a decent little park, and even rudimentary mail service. A few more rusted-out cargo containers were thrown away by the shipping company every month, and travelers always came to claim them as home. The days were long gone that everyone knew everyone's face and name. But they were still society's cast-offs, first skirting the census and then fully ignored by it. That made them family.

"Mark told me to send you to see him. That's all I know."

She knew much more than that. Cutter saw it in the way she held her shoulders, head, and hands. He saw it the way she looked at him, and that wasn't just their history together.

He nodded his gratitude, then turned to run.

"Cutter?"

He looked back.

"I'm sorry."

He ran full-out. Something about Dorothy's sympathy was a blade in his heart. Running the swap gave her authority. Trades often came under dispute, and Dorothy always arbitrated. What she said was how things went. *I'm sorry* from her was like hearing an unassailable mountain crumble.

As unfathomable as Boots dying in the first place.

Shouts came at Cutter as he ran, but fewer than usual. People knew what this was. Just as Dorothy usually kept a stone countenance, he walked without expression or hurry. For Cutter Dunn to break beyond a trot, something must be wrong. He felt his mask of sorrow, didn't much like the pitiful expressions coming from onlookers and friends.

When Boots first came here, as one of the originals,

Amenity had only been ten containers. There'd been no settlement, just Intercoastal United's garbage. It was cheaper for the company to buy new containers than to fix the old ones, and dumping regulations in this part of the country waved the flag of convenience and bribery.

Amenity's first settlers weren't too good for what others saw as trash. For lawmakers, ghost settlements were embarrassing eyesores, but for the ghosts themselves, repurposed housing was as much a matter of pride as repurposing anything else.

It was Intercoastal, not the people, who were foolish to throw away decent shelter. The farthest anyone would need to run could be covered in less than a minute in the early days, but now from the swap to McKenzie's on the far opposite end was over a mile and usually covered in a gas-converted golf cart. Boots, of course, lived in the center. The three or so minutes it took for Cutter to reach his place felt like an eternity.

Time yawned in slow motion. Cutter found himself mining the details of everything he passed. The Gundersons' mailbox was a hollowed-out toaster atop a four-by-four, its old coils repurposed as the family's hotplate. Grease-clotted gears, covered in a tarp, formed the east wall of the Bolshov place because that side of their container had been little more than red dust (and the only spot left) when the Bolshovs arrived.

Inside Winnie Farrow's place, little Desenia was sitting on a dusty area rug, nudging a clockwork frog built by her older brother out of clock springs and sliders from an old audio mixing board. The shells of flat-screen TVs, defunct and scavenged for the rechargeable power cells that used to be inside, formed the borders of the community garden.

And inside Cutter's head, old memories played out. He saw the streets as they were when he was little: smaller, but not as stripped-back as in Boots' first days. He remembered riding a homemade tricycle down the dusty avenues. He remembered his mother, though only barely; she'd gone so early that Cutter was left with only a scene and a feeling.

He didn't remember his father at all and had no idea if he'd ever asked his mother about him. He'd asked Boots, but Boots gave only one response, as enigmatic as the man himself: *Couldn't say*.

Cutter could have pressed, but by the time he turned eighteen, he figured that nothing could come from his history now. Boots was his real parent; Boots *couldn't say* what had come before. To Cutter, that made it irrelevant. Life happened *now*, only *right now*, and nowhere was that truer than Amenity.

The past didn't matter, and the future was wide open. The past was zero, and the future infinity. That's how Boots saw life, and therefore how Cutter preferred to see it, too.

And really, that's why Cutter never went on far-off, months-long rambles the way Boots did right into old age. He never saw the point. Boots said that anything could happen tomorrow, and although to him that meant a person should head out into the world to find it, Cutter thought it meant he should absolutely stay home.

Anything can happen.

And more than not, it did. Amenity was and had always been a magic place rich with goings-on and (to Boots, anyway) irrelevant history. Most people called it a slum, and the people who lived there were poor ... but to Cutter growing up, it was all there ever was and all there could ever be.

He slapped the flap of Boots' door wide as if it had offended him. Boots' shipping container had rusted with age, and to solve it, Boots had put smaller cargo boxes inside his home instead of fixing its shell. His bedroom — his convalescence, recently — was also for cargo: in this case, a Delta Airlines luggage container, about the size of a small bathroom.

Cutter found Boots inside, smoking a cigar.

"You're kidding, right?" he asked his grandfather.

"No. Not yet." Boots looked small as he lay beneath his blankets, but he hadn't lost the sparkle in his eyes. His dark, wrinkled skin reminded Cutter of an old leather boot. He'd never asked if that's where the old man had gotten his nickname. Now the old eyes squinted, focusing. "Okay. Got one: Take my wife …"

"You shouldn't be smoking. Give me that."

"*Please*," Boots finished. Then he held the cigar Groucho Marx style and tapped it like a punchline indicator. The crowd failed to applaud.

Cutter snatched the cigar. Boots used to take care of him; now, their roles were reversed. The transition had proven easier than he'd expected.

"You never heard of Henny Youngman?"

"Jesus, Boots." Cutter was unselfconsciously grabbing blood-spotted handkerchiefs (born as shop towels) that would never come clean. "You should have called before now."

Boots devolved into a coughing fit. It went on too long, and when it ended, Cutter had one more handkerchief to take for attempted laundering.

Then he saw the cards. Boxes and boxes of cards scavenged long ago from an unauthorized trash dump not far away: literally hundreds of packs tossed by one of the casinos.

Boots didn't like things to go to waste, so he'd gone about learning to be a card mechanic (he hated "sleight-of-

SEAN PLATT & JOHNNY B. TRUANT

hand artist" because despite the word "artist," he found the term undignified) just so the cards would stop being useless and start being useful again. When Boots was younger, his abilities had been legendary. He kept trying to teach Cutter because he said a rambling man needed a way to make money while far from home, and scamming card games had always greased his wheels.

But Cutter had no desire to ramble the way Boots always had (and probably his father; Cutter Senior had probably rambled a baby into Mary Jo's belly before rambling away again), and if he needed money, he'd work for it.

Boots found this answer both hilarious and naive. Cutter, because his self-respect demanded it, kept insisting a job was the way. You weren't supposed to cheat in life. If a man played fair with the world, the world would play fair back at him. Problem was, Boots tipped the scales too early. His first memory was stealing a box full of broken machine parts, or so he'd told Cutter more than once.

"I guess I shouldn't know Henny Youngman either," Boots said as Cutter rearranged his bedding. "He played the violin."

"You're supposed to be resting. Not smoking and shuffling cards."

"Or maybe he just held the violin. Did he play it? You tell me."

"I don't have any idea what you're talking about."

"Why you here, boy? Tell me that, and I'll agree to settle."

"Dorothy told me."

"Yeah? What Dorothy tell you? That there's somewhere over the rainbow?"

"What?"

"Fuckin' kids."

"She said you're … " Cutter hedged.

Then Boots started coughing again, and this time he couldn't stop. By the end of his fit, the exhalations were scraping against his internal walls.

"I'll get Sal," Cutter said.

But Boots waved the idea away. "Don't bug Sal. It's too late for that. Sal's been. Been and gone. Lucy K's baby's got something — mumps, maybe. Baby's the future. I'm a used-up old man. You tell me, boy. You tell me if it's worth his time to patch this sinking ship."

Cutter stared into his eyes until the tears started to sting. He had to turn his head so the old man couldn't see. Boots had cried plenty, including in front of Cutter, but the last thing he'd want on his deathbed was to see his grandson spilling tears for him.

It wasn't that it was too sentimental or that sentiment was unnecessary. It was a more practical matter for Boots. Amenity made its life scavenging, repurposing, getting extra lives out of objects the bigger world saw as garbage. You grew up here, and you patched what could be salvaged, and if it couldn't be fixed, you turned the thing into something else.

Clothing became insulation. Clocks stripped small and became watches. Rugs became roofing. Batteries could be sucked far drier than most people thought; Amenity's best minds had found a way.

And it was in that context, now, that Boots was dying.

He was a sweater too threadbare for insulation. He was a battery from which no more charge could be taken. Boots, like anything here, had been squeezed like a sponge, every fraction of value and use wrung from his old bones. He'd reached far past his warranty, far past scrapyard value.

Of course, he had to die. Everyone died. But that

SEAN PLATT & JOHNNY B. TRUANT

didn't mean that Cutter, who'd grown up with Boots as both mother and father, had to like it.

"Oh now," Boots said, seeing Cutter despite his best efforts, "none of that."

"You'll be fine. It's just a coughing fit."

"Like hell." He coughed again, and the end became a phlegmy rattle, like dragging a skeleton through a puddle of drying paint. "Now listen. You wanna be sad? I ain't gonna tell you no. You always did what you always did, and you gonna do what you always done. But when you're finished bein' sad, you gonna promise you'll do something for me, Young Cutter Dunn."

Boots had always had nicknames for him, but he'd never called Cutter exactly that, exactly those three words in that order. *Young Cutter Dunn.* It reminded him that Boots, whose name was also Cutter, was *Old Cutter Dunn.* "Okay. Anything."

His scoff almost invited a fresh coughing fit, but instead, Boots rolled and waited until the spasm passed. In the new position, Cutter could see his stuck-out collarbone and visible ribs. He was suddenly much, much older than he'd always been — and ready for that great recycling heap in the sky.

"*Anything?* Don't agree before you know what you're agreeing to, fool. Or maybe it don't matter. Because you're gonna do this anyway. You're gonna because it's an old man's last wish. You're gonna do it because if you don't, I'm gonna haunt 'cha."

That sussed a bittersweet smile from Cutter. "Okay. Then tell me."

"You gonna ramble. That's what you gonna do."

"Okay."

Boots actually hit him on the arm. His exertions, in the seconds after Cutter's agreement, shouldn't have been possible. "Don't you sass me! Don't you lie, Cutter Dunn. You don't get ta say *Okay* and think the senile old man'll just believe it. Don't bullshit a bullshitter, boy. I seen both coasts. I been around more poker tables than you got hairs on your sack. I know when someone's feeding me crap or takin' pity and tellin' me what they think I wanna hear."

"Hey, I—"

"*I. I.* Yeah, I heard your *I*'s plenty. When you snuck off to Lily's place when you was fourteen, over and over, every time I caught you, and I had you dead to rights, and you'd just stammer like an idiot. 'Boots, I—' An I always cut you off. 'Cept once. I jes wanted to see what you'd say if I let you go. But there wasn't anything else, was there? So, you finally gonna finish that sentence. I-*what*? That's your problem: You don't know. You lived here on my titty and this place's titty, and sure you done good work but that right there's the problem, don't you see? You stay in Amenity now, you gonna stay forever. It's too comfortable. Someone here'll always need you, so it ain't really your choice, then, right? You *gotta* stay!"

He laughed and coughed. "Well. Let us be clear, you and me. You look me in the eyes right now, Cutter. You look me in the eyes so ain't no confusion about what I'm gonna say. Come on, now."

He leaned in. The old man's eyes were raisins in yellowed pools, the works wrapped in stiff and wrinkled blankets.

"You listening?"

Cutter nodded.

"You go. You head to the yard, and you hop on any train. Don't even need to know where. Pack your cleanest clothes, stuff to shower and smell clean, and the cash you got saved. Not many folks pay with it anymore, but people will still take it, and it spends just fine. Folks are gonna look at you funny when none'a the screens read the chip you don't got, but our kind has been seen before. You got a good head and a strong back. You can fix things better than ol' Boots ever did. The world still needs those skills; don't you let anyone tell you otherwise. You're too big for this place. You hear me?"

"But this is … home," Cutter said.

"It's where you were born. 'Home' is where you make it. Don't get me wrong. Amenity's good folks. But the world ain't what people say it is 'round here, Cutter. That's something you need to know before your old pops heads out on his final ramble. The world ain't against us. It ain't to be scared of. I can see your *real* life, Cutter, 'cause I been out there, and I know there's a hole, somewhere, for a man like you to grow into."

"I'm not part of their system, Boots. None of us are."

He coughed again, flagging fast, but Cutter refused to turn from it. Boots had always made his own rules and never let anyone tell him otherwise … this last gasp wouldn't be different.

"You're right. You're none 'o their system. But that's good, don't you see? They gonna feel sorry for you. They maybe gonna spit on you sometimes. I won't lie. But way things is out there, there's no real ingenuity left. No creativity. They're in the box, and you're outside it. You use that brain of yours the way I know you can" — he leaned all the way forward and tapped Cutter's head — "and you'll see. You play straight with the world, and it'll play straight with you. I'm makin' you a promise, you get me? You stand up for yourself the way people here have their pride, and sooner or later, you gonna shine."

Cutter had his doubts. But then again, the books in their extensive library said explorers once had doubts about sailing far and wide, unsure if they might sail them-

22

selves off the ends of the world. It had taken guts to venture out then. It would take guts — not just competence, of which Cutter had great supply — to venture out now.

Boots took his hand. "You promise me. Go out and then, if you want, you can come home. Promise me you'll try. Amenity's been here almost thirty years. It ain't goin' nowhere soon, and it'll be just fine while you're gone. But —" He squeezed Cutter's hand harder, and then his face and voice became less of its hectoring self and more pleading. "But you tell me now you'll go, son. You tell me now, and I'll believe you just fine."

"Okay." A tear licked Cutter's cheek, then fell onto his arm. "Okay, Boots. I promise."

The old man sighed, smiled, and closed his eyes.

It wasn't long after that, as if a *yes* was all he'd been waiting for.

Chapter Three

AND SO IT WENT.

The day after Boots was gone, Cutter said his goodbyes and realized right away that his grandfather had seen something Cutter somehow never had: Amenity was part of Cutter's soul, but he'd somehow detached himself from it long ago without ever being the wiser.

He'd lived among his neighbors but had never tied himself to anyone. He'd never gotten married and barely dated. Boots was his only kin, if he even *was* kin, and after Boots was in the ground, Cutter found himself with hardly any attachments at all. Dorothy might have been the only thing that could have kept him him there, but that ship had sailed, and besides, she was capable of taking care of herself and Amenity while Cutter was gone. Same as when he was there.

There were formal jobs inside Amenity's settlement if you wanted to call them that, with payment made by barter. Even in a community of outcasts and loners, Cutter cast himself out by constantly doing his own thing. He was liked, of course — maybe even loved. But when time came to leave, he found himself without a single entanglement.

Seemed he wasn't an inseparable cog of the settlement after all. Cutter was more like the module you slap onto the outside of a functioning machine. It improved things, sure, but you could always remove the module, and the machine would keep right on running just fine.

Still, he packed with trepidation, taking longer than he needed. Cutter had his life inside a backpack in no time, baffled by the speed at which he lifted right out of Amenity. It was as if he'd been packed for years without ever knowing it. Maybe Boots was right. Maybe he'd always been a rambling man … too scared of what was out there to do it right.

You play straight with the world, and it'll play straight with you. I'm makin' you a promise, you get me?

The old man's words of wisdom would have felt like a crutch if Boots were still alive: a kid insisting his mother hold his hand until he was safe in his seat on the school bus. But with his grandfather gone to the Great Beyond, they felt more like a memorial. Homage, even. Cutter took comfort in them, repeating them like a mantra in his head, trying to believe as Boots had.

There was great distrust and fear inside Amenity about the wider world, but according to Boots, technology didn't turn humans into something else. Money could corrupt, but it couldn't change a person's brains or DNA.

In the cities, from the videos they'd all seen and stories people like Boots told, all the machines knew who you were. People who'd been born with credentials had keys to those machines and needed little more than to go about their business while the computers took care of them.

But were they not still humans beneath it all? Cutter

chose to believe they were. His lack of official identity papers made him what people in the cities called a "ghost." Plenty of places had their own superstitions about the uncredentialed (the worst said they were like dead souls walking), but plenty of others had none. The world was not black and white, said Boots.

There were not cities on one side and places like Amenity on the other. In between those extremes were smaller settlements where each understood the other. Cutter just had to find them and offer his skills. The first job would be the hardest, but then he'd adjust, and the second would surely be easier.

His first stop was in a town called Moorsdale, an hour down the East-West line. It was the first populated area that struck Cutter as more than a ghost settlement yet was far less glitzy than the videos he'd seen.

He hopped off the rattler, then hiked into town, shouldering his pack. He was self-conscious immediately. Locals drove automobiles — electric and charged by the sun — instead of ancient golf carts that had been battered to nothing.

And now here, Cutter was coming into town like a true rambler ... but upon reaching the first crossroads, he found himself overreacting. There were plenty of people on foot, and a few had backpacks. Cutter had shaved before embarking and had his hair cut. Clean and combed, at first, he didn't stand out at all. He could live here happily despite the noise.

He went first to the local hardware store, seeing as tools were one thing he knew well. The man initially showed interest in hiring Cutter, but then they entered the back room to sit and talk, and the refrigerator only rotated a single water to the front instead of a bottle for each of them. The man sat him down to watch the store's orientation video, but the screens wouldn't respond to Cutter's presence.

"I'm sorry, but I can't hire anyone undocumented. I don't own the place, you understand? If auditors decided to pay us a visit … "

The man seemed genuinely sorry. Cutter smiled and told him it was no problem, then left with a *thanks*. He was pleased, despite the rejection. Now he knew the lay of the land. The computers weren't psychic; they were useful. They didn't read minds or plunge souls; screens seemed to recognize faces while ubiquitous scanners read some sort of implants under their wrists.

Seeing it in action stripped the mystery for Cutter, which dulled his trepidation and fear. Described, larger society had sounded like black magic. Now, he saw it was just another set of machines.

Cutter couldn't program computers, and he'd never met anyone who could. But they were made of wires and glass and parts he did understand, and what remained above his knowledge were things he could learn if he cared enough. He wouldn't fit in here and now understood why these people called his kind ghosts.

In a real sense, those without chipped-and-confirmed government identities could only exist halfway in places like this. But Moorsdale wasn't bad in that way at all. It was still close to Amenity and other similar villages, so the ghosts weren't so scary.

But the hardware store rejection also taught Cutter something else. Just as Boots said, his value was clear. The proprietor *had* wanted to hire him, even after knowing he had no official census credentials, and that meant others would want to hire him as well. He even fixed an old radio before leaving: not a stock item, but a century-old antique sitting on the manager's desk.

"Nobody here had any idea how to do that," he told Cutter in disbelief. "If you can't find what's wrong using a diagnostic pad, most folks will give up and throw something away."

Throw something away.

Boots was turning over in his grave. The radio wasn't even hard to fix, and they were just going to toss it. His eyes were opened to the true waste of this world, fully understanding for the first time why pickings, even for what the government called "rats" in their ghost colonies, were always so abundant.

They could repair nothing. Tried to repair nothing. Most of what Cutter saw, even in appliance stores, was disposable. The things could read your face and know your preferences, and a washer could monitor the detergent levels in nearby cupboards, and everything was tied to everything, and not a single bit of that "everything" would respond to *Cutter's* face, *Cutter's* touch, *Cutter's* lack of a registry chip.

But Cutter didn't care. So little relied on the computer. Washing machines still had to spin and agitate, moving large parts around belts and gears. Automobiles could drive themselves for the most part, but their wheels still turned on axles — and even though the steering wheel wasn't connected to the drive train, *something* was connected to it. Cutter quickly discovered that machines remained machines no matter how "smart" they became, and even the ubiquitous screens that failed to recognize Cutter when he passed still had wires that could be soldered and buttons to push.

There was plenty for Cutter Dunn here. And not just

work he *could* do, but work he came quickly to feel he *had* to do because no one else could. He had value, more worth in the outside world than back home.

He traveled and worked. Traveled and worked. He was a moving target, never in one place too long because Boots was his omnipresent companion.

Work came slowly at first. Initially, he took manual labor: shoveling at a landscaping company, loading grain bags into customers' cars at a feed dispensary, washing dishes in a diner.

Upon parlaying his recommendations into machine-assisted labor, Cutter started running forklifts to load trucks, startled to learn that the vehicles were computers on wheels. As long as the forklift job lasted, in a burg called Slater's Cove, Cutter learned all he could about the trucks he spent his days packing. Once orientation ended, he had no supervisor and didn't need one; the trucks themselves told him what to do.

Load higher. More. Less. Distribute load for proper weight-balancing. Inflate tires. Deflate tires. Shift draft shields to improve fuel efficiency.

Once Cutter crawled under one of his charges and, with the help of a robotic jack he didn't remotely understand, replaced a damaged differential. The next morning, it was as if he'd revealed himself as a wizard.

It was simple, Cutter insisted. *No problem at all.*

They'd had all the parts, and the truck had told him it couldn't roll until the part was fixed. He wasn't about to ignore it. And yet, his manager was flabbergasted. Acted like Cutter had launched a man to the moon and back.

He stayed in each town long enough to get bored before moving on. It was particularly hard to leave his fork-lift job, especially after they moved him to active repair duty when needed, but the problem in every city was ultimately the same: beyond a certain pay threshold, the companies he worked for had to document their outgoings. Doing so required identifications Cutter didn't have and numerical scans he would never possess.

In some cities (and Slater's Cove was one of those cities), questionable dealers offered to give Cutter the ID he lacked.

Happens all the time, they all explained to him. *People come, and people go. Sometimes someone needs credentials for the census, and just so happens someone else died and left theirs available. The government doesn't even mind. It turns a blind eye because they want the taxes.*

Cutter always said no thank you. Boots was in his head, offering a simpler solution: restart the clock at least one town over. He didn't like the idea of suddenly being part of the system, especially illegally so. He had a ghost's deep suspicion of order and tracking in his blood, preferring to remain his own man. He had no strings. Or attachments. And that's how he liked it.

Until Cutter reached a moderate-sized city on the edge of an industrial zone called Prosperity. There he landed a run-down but clean rental in a widow's basement and a job at a shipping hub for a major online merchant.

Ever since the Cove, Cutter had gravitated toward anything transportation-related. It'd taken only a lone glimpse at the depot from a hilltop to see its shape: a pair of twin *L's* conjoined by a central section, the entire outline pocked by trucks assembled for loading.

"What would you think," Cutter asked the manager after his third successful week on the job, "if I tried learning to drive those trucks?"

The manager's answer was the last thing Cutter expected.

"Drive the trucks? Kid, those are smart trucks. A

person goes with them just to be sure, but mostly they drive themselves."

It was all he needed to hear.

Cutter was already in love.

Chapter Four

THE HUB'S manager was a man named Gord. Cutter had no idea if it was his first or last name, or maybe just a nickname. He knew only that everyone called him Gord and that he looked like a Gord. His face and neck were one sloping mound, and his shirt was always untucked despite the fact that it was a dress shirt and meant to look neat. His face was black from the nose down by 3pm, as if his beard was forever itching to get started. There was usually — not always, but often — dried food spatter on his shoe.

On the day the Hollander Sitwell representatives came for training, Gord stood very close to Cutter. "I'm vouching for you. If it comes down to it, I'm swiping for you." He indicated his own wrist. "And not just 'cause I like you. Though I do like you, Cutter. It's 'cause this place is a bleeding shithole. Literally. This place is some monster's big old butthole, and it's got a fissure, and every day around here, it's just shit and blood."

"Hell, Gord," Cutter said.

"Because you gotta understand. It's not my fault the

goddamn roof's caving in. It's not my fault the owner's a cock. I can't fight City Hall any better than you."

Cutter failed to see what fighting City Hall had to do with it but kept his mouth shut.

"Revenue drops anymore, and they'll fire me. The owner's a cheap prick. He's also a cock."

And the facility was a bleeding rectum? Gord's only metaphors were about unmentionable body parts.

"I keep tellin' him, Hollander's our biggest client. More-a their trucks unload here than anywhere else. But you know what they're talkin' now? Building their own hub. Or not bothering with one. They got this new thing. You'll hear all about it in a sec." Gord tapped his head, implying intellectualism that Cutter didn't really think he had. "I pay attention. Sure they're shipping all sorts of stuff, but these days it's windshields windshields windshields."

"Windshields?"

"Smart windshields. Every smart windshield you ever seen on a car or a truck, Hollander Sitwell probably made it."

Cutter didn't know what a smart windshield was, so he had no idea if he'd seen one. He nodded along anyway.

"My new car's got one. Pain in the ass if you ask me. I go in my car to escape shit, not to spend all my time on it. Now my wife is constantly calling. I get messages. Fucking LiveLyfe feed. You on LiveLyfe?"

"I don't really know what it is," Cutter told him.

"Oh. Yeah. 'Course you wouldn't. Anyway, these screens. They basically tell you how to drive your own goddamn car."

Cutter assumed this was figurative. Most cars were self-driving, at least on a highway.

"Fuel economy. How fast you're going. How fast

you *gone*. Tied into the police if you ask me. Look at this shit. I'll tell you. Cops pull you over, and they got your speed right on the 'shield. Fucking Big Brother. All the trucks got 'em now. All the Hollander trucks."

"Okay," said Cutter.

"Half the trucks HS used to send through here are now making runs between Vegas and somewhere in Montana. Saw that coming, am I right?"

Cutter didn't understand what anything had to do with anything, but that was normal for Gord.

"Anyway, they can't find mechanics. The trucks are just boxes. It's the tech they care about. Trying to get trucks to drive themselves. And I mean *completely* drive themselves."

"So not just the freeway? Like … a truck could leave one place and pull all the way into another without a driver?"

"Pull in, pull out, maybe even load and unload. Fucking Vegas, man. Vanadium."

Cutter didn't comment.

"Anyway. I got this idea. Branching out. We stop being just a hub. Nobody wants hubs when trucks drive themselves. 'Specially Hollander. Vanadium mine is in Montana, I guess, and they make the windshields outside Vegas. If we just sit here with our fists up our bloody fissuring assholes—"

"Jesus, Gord."

"—then we're gonna be yesterday's news. So here's my idea. Get this. They want folks trained to load and unload their smarty-pants trucks? Cool. We sneak you in. Like I said, I'll scan for you if I have to. Don't matter if you're a fucking ghost or what. You got the best hands I seen, Cutter. Magical. We go in, and we sell 'em on the idea of making us not just a hub, but a repair shop, too. No more need to hunt for mechanics. We fix their shit while they load and unload. Smart, right?"

It *was* smart in the end, but not in the way Gord planned. Cutter did sneak into the training, and Gord did announce his idea, but instead of embracing the notion of turning the hub into a repair shop, Hollander Sitwell embraced Cutter instead. They offered him a job — not at the hub, but in Vegas or wherever in Montana or maybe both. Cutter, loyal, took Hollander's offer to Gord, who shrugged.

"Just as well. I looked into it, and we can't hire you long-term anyway." Gord offered him a heavy sigh. "Winky there said he can bring you on. Payroll. You wanna grab that shit, you do it."

So Cutter did. The man Gord had called "Winky" was actually named Robert Stockton, Jr., not to be confused with Robert Stockton, Sr. — "I'm my own man, Mr. Dunn. I'm not here because of nepotism, and I can prove it" — and never winked that Cutter saw.

The work was good. Cutter started immediately, working on a line coordinating assembly bots. Within a day, Cutter recognized efficiencies and made them. For one, the AI running the line was far more capable of coordinating the robots than any human, and Cutter, who knew nothing about artificial intelligence, was still able to plug one thing into the other.

He was underused after that, shuffling parts on the line like a monkey. It went on that way for a week until one of the robots broke. Workers were paid by the hour, far outside of union territory, and were about to be sent home without the second half day's pay when Cutter decided to climb over the line and down a maze of conveyors until he reached the problem.

A leaking gasket caused a hydraulic cylinder to lose

pressure. An easy fix requiring five minutes. There was even a quick access ... just one another machine was supposed to use rather than anyone thinking a human could do it. Machines relying on machines ... in Cutter's mind built a house of cards.

The line was moving a quarter-hour later, and the entire staff cheered.

Cutter ascended quickly after the line incident. Hollander Sitwell had solved the problem plaguing all his previous employers — not by issuing him fake credentials but by finding a way to keep an uncredentialed man on their books. It was technically illegal, but they wouldn't tell anyone if he wouldn't.

A bit more poking around, and Cutter decided the company was basically laundering its own money to pay him under the table, but two things about the arrangement made it not matter. He discovered both things by bedding a woman named Holly, who liked him very much and who happened to work in accounting. He wasn't fishing for information, but Holly offered it anyway.

First, money was money. They have to pay him in ducats to make the whole thing work because cash grabbed too much attention ... but that was okay because he could spend ducats just fine, and all he'd heard suggested the system was actually foolproof.

Despite the phantom nature of digital currency, Holly assured Cutter that precise records meant deposited sums were guaranteed; they had reams of documents required by government auditors to ensure that was true. Second, Holly seemed to suggest that Hollander Sitwell did a *lot* with its money where government eyes couldn't see. They weren't breaking laws just for Cutter.

As long as nobody looks too close, it's all invisible. If you don't care that you're technically — and only technically — breaking the law, then nothing will go wrong.

Or so Holly promised.

Cutter remembered what Boots had told him, about his value to the world and the fact that things were fair more often than not. If he treated the company right, they'd treat him right back. He should appreciate the lengths they went to pay him and did.

Soon after, he was moved to be a worker on — and then engineering head of — the V-See Express project.

V-See was fascinating to Cutter. Things were as Gord had predicted. Hollander really was headed full steam into the smart glass market. Their windshields were hot commodities and increasingly a cornerstone of profits, so it only made sense to shift away from other holdings and double-down on heads-up display technology.

The most important material in smart glass manufacture was vanadium, and Hollander Sitwell's chief mine was in Montana. With manufacturing happening in Vegas, the Vegas-Montana truck run became the company's most important artery. Its lifeline to profits, as it were.

Cutter didn't understand how the windshields worked, nor did he need to. He also didn't understand how the next thing his bosses started discussing would work but didn't need to know *that*, either. He was hands and mechanical brains, not their computer guy.

Hollander was already running self-driving trucks, but just as Gord said, they wanted more from those vehicles. In short, the goal was to teach a truck how to successfully pull into the vanadium mine, load, then drive unassisted to the Vegas plant and unload … in under fifty hours.

They were close by the time Cutter came on, but the gap between "close" and "complete" was larger than it looked. To Hollander's people, the system seemed only to need a few tweaks. Right now, the trucks were *almost* unmanned; a driver rode shotgun to the AI and only touched the controls if something went wrong — or, for now, during the start and end of the journey.

To Hollander, a gap of inches remained. To Cutter, it was much more — and *that* was why the company hadn't solved the problem despite thousands of dedicated man-hours.

"Look," Cutter said, pointing to one of a thousand graphs — this one showing wind tunnel testing, "the problem is never here." He indicated the timespan showing the middle of the trip. "It's always here and here."

His most recent boss, Marie, rolled her eyes. She was out on a limb for their lone ghost employee and vanguard for those who, superstitious or not, had been stupid enough to believe the rumors around ghosts. Now Cutter was embarrassing her by stating the obvious.

"I know you know that, but you're thinking like programmers." Cutter had no idea how programmers thought, but it was definitely different than the way he did things, so this seemed enough. "I don't suppose any of you has ever fixed a washing machine."

"Cutter ..." said Marie.

"Hear me out. A belt spins the drum. Fast at the end, to get rid of the water. Right?"

Blank stares. Technically these people had washing machines, but just as technically, they probably had mother systems that removed the necessity for them to actually interact with, load or fix them. Life here was a magical realm where dirty clothes went in, and clean ones came out folded.

"Anything spins fast, you have to worry about load balancing. Same with a wheel on your car. What happens if you run through a big fat patch of tar, and it sticks to one side?" But no one knew. "The wheel wobbles because it's out of balance."

"What's your point?" asked a tall man named Jaxon, with an X. "Our trucks don't spin."

"No, but you still have to balance the load. Look." Again Cutter pointed at graphs, but this was effectively kabuki; none of them had a clue what he was getting at. "You're using a ton of gas pulling the trailer uphill. Downhill, the engine has to brake. Turns have to be slow, careful, and methodical. Backing up has to be done by feel, which only a human can do because it's too complex an action, moving backward with a big trailer behind a cab."

He shifted documents. "And look how you're loading. From the front to the back. I've worked at a shipping hub. All the goods have to move out from the center. Imagine being able to load from both ends. Or the top. Robots could do that kind of thing easy, and the truck would just have to pull alongside or underneath."

"You're talking about redesigning the entire process," Jaxon argued. "It'd cost millions."

"Tens of millions," added someone else.

"Some redesign of the facilities would be needed, yes. Definitely a redesign of the trucks, but go back to the unbalanced load thing. The finesse points — the parts of the trip that still require human drivers — all come from this clumsy design. I'm talking about the raw material, about the engineering mess you're building from in the first place. Not anything created by Hollander Sitwell."

"You mean the trucks themselves?" Marie asked. "Plain old eighteen-wheelers."

He nodded. "Hard to drive. Hard to back. Hard to steer. Wide turns, unidirectional loading … no wonder we can't make it work."

"So what do you suggest?" asked a higher-up who was

clearly asking semi-rhetorically, sure Cutter — this Johnny-come-lately *ghost* of all stupid things — had no real answer of value.

"Remove the cab."

It was like Cutter had shouted a slur.

"What?" Marie finally said.

"Remove the cab. Run a trailer by itself, and put the engine in the middle."

"Jesus," replied the higher-up. "Thanks for playing, Marie."

But Marie seemed to get it — or at least the start of what Cutter was saying. "How would it steer?"

"We used to do this kind of thing racing junk buggies back home. If an HS truck without any cab was my starter for a junk buggy, I'd put a double-double of drive wheels in the middle, each five to ten feet from the engine's center of gravity. Both sets would pivot three-sixty and act as drive wheels."

"Fuck's sake. What, you want it to be able to do pirou-ettes?" Jaxon asked.

Aware he was being mocked but equally sure his idea was better than anything else on the table, Cutter raised an eyebrow. "Two sets of dually drive wheels in the middle, then passive wheels near either end. It'd be like nothing on the road but maneuverable as hell compared to what's out there now. You could design a hub to load from both ends at once, buttressing the engine, or you could top-load like a grain car. Vanadium can be poured instead of shipped in barrels and should be."

Marie was studying the idea, making sketches on a whiteboard. "There's no way to send a driver along for test runs. What if something goes wrong?"

Cutter had already considered that. "Drivers need to sit up front where they can see the road. But you don't need that, do you? Drones fly unmanned all the time. Put your driver in something like a simulator until you trust the system. They can take over remotely if needed. They don't need to be inside the actual truck. It's all fly-by-wire anyway."

Jaxon-with-an-X rubbed his chin, reluctant to admit anything positive. But there was profit to be had, and he knew it. "This will require a ton of testing. Little adjustment. That can't be done remotely."

"Right. But not by a driver. You need a technician aboard to fix things. You need a mechanic, not a sack of meat to sit up front. You want someone able to respond immediately, fix problems as they occur, be your eyes on board until all the kinks are worked out.

Jaxon waved at Marie's crude drawing — a hand flap of surrender. "But there's nowhere for them to sit or lay down. Fifty hours. No cab. No windows. No way to brake or steer if the drone link craps out. No stops, no seat ... no sleep. Who the hell wants to do that?"

The room was silent, but only for seconds.

Cutter had planned for this one, too. "I'll do it."

Chapter Five

QUARTERS WERE HOT. Smelly. Thick and humid as balls, and for some reason, Cutter hadn't considered that inside a giant moving rectangle (not all that different from a shipping container home in Amenity, though packed with crystals of vanadium), there'd be no room for heat to escape.

In addition, Hollander Sitwell's chemists had informed Cutter that he should really wear a respirator if he planned to ride so close to the cargo because vanadium pentoxide could result in lung damage. He was grateful for the protection but re-breathing his own air and snugging his exhales so close to his face only made everything hotter.

The safety officer had, at least, insisted Cutter have some protection. On the test voyages, instead of keeping the engine compartment in the trailer's center as small as possible to maximize the load, the central chamber was more than twice as spacious as it would be in the final design, the engine itself accessible from inside the truck instead of just the outside as required by the final specs.

This had the benefit of keeping Cutter from being crushed by vanadium once the truck reached the mine and took on its payload, but the significant disadvantage of having a giant engine as his roommate. It was, of course, electric, not diesel, though there were times Cutter wished it *was* diesel despite the asphyxiation risk. Diesel was loud and dirty and smelly, but electric engines felt like they were always waiting to arc out and fry you.

But even besides that, diesel struck Cutter as more honest. He didn't trust the electric hum, like a transformer farm, for over two days of nonstop travel. During his spare time at the old hub, Gord had let him work out how to drive an ancient diesel truck on the lot that had a thirty-inch stick shift — a beast with no home on modern roads seeing as the alloys used in its manufacture created electromagnetic echoes, meaning tracking systems and ID dongles (necessary to avoid collisions and protect civilian drivers) could not be installed.

To Cutter, this shortcoming made him and the truck copacetic. They were both ghosts. Neither were seen by the civilized world. They were outcasts … and temperamental or not, Cutter liked the old thing just fine.

The electric engine burned clean because it didn't burn at all, the works fueled by an array of enormous batteries on the truck's front and back like counterweights. But its moving parts sweltered, so although he found a way to jam a bolted-down chair into his moving coffin, Cutter didn't want to sit in it. Once underway, he flaunted safety regs by climbing above the holdback walls around him and popping the central fill hatch, then climbing out with a harness on and a short security line holding him to grab the handles topside. He rode that way for far more than those back in Vegas would have liked … but Cutter also knew where there were cameras and where there weren't.

There was a long trip to Montana from Vegas. The vanadium hopper jammed, and Cutter had to poke it with a literal broom, technically nullifying the trip as "fully automated," but nobody needed to know that. By now, the news outlets — and Hollander Sitwell's competitors — were watching.

Otherwise, the load end, modified close to on-the-fly and improving in the coming weeks, worked admirably well. So too on the unload end, but there were too many glitches in the trip's middle to fool anyone. The remote driver took over twice — once to avoid a rather nasty head-on collision caused by false identification of another truck by the AI running it. He had to adjust the engine four separate times while the rig was moving. It was running too fast and failing to cool. Problems with the code, he was told.

And so it went. For six months, Cutter's only job was to ride trucks back and forth: Vegas to Montana, Montana to Vegas. The truck's armpit was his home on the road. There was no bed on the Montana end; the whole venture was meant to prove Vegas and back was feasible by AI alone, meaning there needn't be a human break. He had to fight hard for two nights between rides — Jaxon, in particular, wanted just one day between — and stayed at a quaint B&B run by a grandmother named June and her daughter July.

"Of course, those are really our names. Who could make this stuff up?"

By the second month after redesigning the first truck, executives were optimistic that it was only a matter of time.

By four months, they'd already lost all that optimism and had begun yelling at Cutter to do it better, do it faster, do it right.

By five months, Cutter had started to hear chatter

about how maybe the ghost wasn't worth what they were paying him. He delved deeper and worked harder.

Two days into the fifth month, an order came down that Cutter didn't need nights off between hauls. The truck certainly didn't.

So they sent him out again and again, and when Cutter complained, Marie suggested that maybe he should keep his mouth shut. He was a below-the-table employee who'd seen and heard much of the company's dirtier laundry and technically wasn't supposed to be working without credentials anyway.

News of what HS was trying to do had spread far and wide, and already the company was worried people might learn who they'd hired. Human resources got in touch, suggested Cutter maybe do as former employers had suggested and forge himself some papers. He finally told them to go ahead and start the process. It would take even more time — months again — but at least the news folks could be allowed to see him without harm.

Until then, keeping Cutter inside the truck and rolling at all times served a dual purpose. He was out of sight and thus out of scrutiny. Because he had no credentials, news drones and other onlookers following the pilot trucks couldn't scan them to report what was inside. Hollander Sitwell said the vehicles were already unmanned, not operated by one dedicated mechanic, and pointed out only the remote driver in the simulator back in Vegas.

To Cutter, this started to feel less like the company protecting him, though they were, and more like a prison. He obviously couldn't go topside with his harness while news drones were watching, so he had to sit in his hot little chair, reading when he could, drinking plenty of water, and peeing in a jug while passing the time.

"But just think," said a vice president Cutter met with during the worst of it. "You're getting rich. We pay for meals, and you don't need lodging. Your salary is the highest we've ever paid someone in your position. And we're getting close. This is *close*, Mr. Dunn; can you feel it?"

"I guess."

"You're unhappy. You're burned out."

Cutter shrugged.

"Okay. I understand. I want to help you. But the goddamn drones are everywhere. We're sort of painted into a corner. You know how the news thinks the trucks are unmanned? Well, they do. And now we're committed. Anyone sees you entering or leaving one of our prototypes, it's over. I know you're a mechanic, and I know you're just making tweaks on the road." He put a splayed hand on his breast. "*I* know that. Others don't. Think of how it would look if anyone knew — and without your papers. You understand?"

"Sort of."

"Good, good. Now. Is there anything I can do? Anything at all. Anything other than letting you outside or telling the world you exist."

There was one thing. Cutter had gotten word from Dorothy. She was expecting her first baby, but reading between the lines, it seemed like she was having some trouble. Amenity supported its community, but there was only so much its citizens could do. Dorothy needed a better doctor than they could provide. There was a decent hospital not far off that took ghost patients and allowed them to pay cash since none of them had the credentials for more contemporary ducats. She just needed to *get* the cash. Fortunately, Cutter was willing to bet he had a lot more than he needed.

"How much money do I have saved up?" Cutter asked the VP.

"You don't know?"

Again he shrugged. "I'm paid in ducats. I've been told I can withdraw it in cash." Cutter rushed on. "Not right now, of course."

"No, no, not right now. That would raise big red flags."

"So how much do I have? I was told the company kept the records."

The VP looked at a screen. "Looks like just shy of fifty thousand."

Cutter's jaw dropped. Ducats to dollars was around one-to-one, and Cutter had never before in his life held more than a hundred at one time. "You sure?"

The VP handed Cutter a paper.

"What's this?"

"Proof." He pointed. "That's your wallet ID. Coded, of course. HR should have given you the corresponding key. Run one through the other, and you'll get a federal seal verifying your balance."

Cutter reached for the paper, but the VP pulled it back, adopting the air of someone who'd made a mistake.

"Sorry. That's the wrong one."

"Wrong how?" Cutter had seen his name on it.

"It's just a different copy."

"But a copy. Meaning the same."

"Sure. But … It's complicated. Talk to HR. They'll talk to Records."

"Isn't it all online? Can't I just check it myself?"

"Of course, just …" And then the VP ended his sentence with a whole lot of shit Cutter had never heard before and didn't understand, now or ever. Computer stuff.

Things he couldn't do or comprehend because he'd been born a ghost and was scheduled to die as one.

Cutter was a liability, but that would change once his documentation was in place. Then he could leave the facility all he wanted. He could run around in public. The world would see him as valid, and real, and visible, and maybe he'd even get credit as the innovator who made an amazing thing possible.

Probably would. Yes, it was a company invention, but HS had shared employee credit in the past.

But for now, none of it solved his problem. "I need you to do a favor for me if you really want to help."

"Sure, sure," said the VP.

"Take ten thousand of my ducats. Turn it into cash."

"Sure. Sure."

"Then send it—" Cutter could do so much better than just Dorothy with ten grand. "Send it to the undocumented settlement of Amenity, with half specifically earmarked for Dorothy Malko." This seemed to need justification. "She's pregnant."

"Oh. I see." A sly, insulting grin bloomed on the VP's face. "Left a little bundle back home, did you? A man's gotta cover his tracks."

"That's not what this is. Her guy is gone, but I'd have never left what was mine.

"Sure, sure," the VP said.

The work continued. At almost exactly the six-month mark, Cutter found himself sweating down his ass crack inside a truck that had managed, on its own, to pull out of the Vegas lot, drive all the way to the mine, load up without help, then pull out and head home.

It was the farthest the venture had gotten. He was halfway to Vegas, with traffic and weather forecasts free and clear. It just had to pull in, center over the main hopper, and open its bottom so gravity could do the rest.

It was cake. And they were going to make it.

But then his radio crackled — never a good sign, with the remote driver on the line. "Cutter. You there, Cutter?"

"Abed. Jesus. Don't do this to me."

"No, no," he scrambled to say, though Abed's tone was anything but pacific. "I haven't touched the controls. Nothing's gone wrong."

A long pause. "Yet."

"What is it?"

"I think one of the spark plugs is bad. And—"

Cutter exhaled. "That's fine. It can run without one."

"I wasn't finished. It's bad because it's fouled with oil. Which, okay, fine. But on my end, I'm seeing a serious oil leak. *That's* the problem. The plug is just the symptom. And Cutter? We're already really low."

Cutter exhaled. This was just more evidence of dead-end thinking over long-term sense. Ever since Tesla, electric engines hadn't needed conventional oil. Or spark plugs, for that matter. But of course, even with such a vital project, HS had cut all kinds of corners, arguing that a diesel engine converted to electric was just as good as a from-zero electric engine, and the project was already insanely over budget with (in their eyes) *little improvement per additional dollar spent.*

Now that decision would bite everyone. Stupid assholes were still introducing sparks and sludge to the mix when those problems were easy to avoid. And worse, this was probably his last chance to prove himself.

Monetary allocations were doled out monthly — and Cutter had already been told, contrary to all evidence obvious to patient, science-minded people, that the project was considered a boondoggle and a coming failure. Too many news stories about how the HUD and smart wind-shield manufacturer was blowing the success (and share-holder value) it had banked by bleeding tens or hundreds of millions into their dead-end smart truck project.

To Cutter, what he'd worked for every day represented unassailable progress. To the suits, it was somehow a quixotic endeavor with no redeeming value. Baffling, but perfectly corporate.

"We need to fix it," Cutter said.

"Fine. The engine's not redlining just yet. My guess is you've still got oil enough for another fifty miles. Think you can make it to the service station up near Fortsmund?"

Abed didn't sound any happier about it than Cutter was. They both knew the stakes, and although nobody had wanted to say the words aloud and drape a pall over the run, in truth, this was the make-or-break test: the last one V-See would get that actually mattered. Hollander Sitwell would likely putter with their smart truck project regard-less, but if today failed, next month's budget for the endeavor would fail, and that, effectively, would be that.

HS was staring down the barrel of a PR nightmare — maybe even hostile board action — if it threw any more good after what it inexplicably saw as bad. Your classic failure to see the bigger picture.

They would succeed now or literally never.

"Abed?"

"Yeah, boss." Abed called him boss even though Cutter wasn't. This one was sad, like surrender.

"You can't take the controls and stop us in Fortsmund."

"Sooner? Give me a minute. I think there's a garage on—"

"No. I mean, you can't take the controls at all."

"What do you mean?"

Cutter took a few long breaths. The engine, louder than any other electric, thanks to all those sparks (and the fact that it wasn't nearly as electric as it should be), counted the beats. "We have to get the truck all the way to Vegas. *Without* you touching the controls."

"Boss. That's … What? Six more hours? It'll overheat. With extreme prejudice. If only—"

"Let it ride, Abed. We can make it."

Cutter knew where Abed was going because he'd been there all day.

Stupid fucking suits with their stupid fucking ways of thinking. Penny wise and pound foolish. It had been fine when it was just the company, or at least better, but then everyone had started paying attention to the smart truck project and making fun of it. Hollander Sitwell bowed to pressure and stockholder demands. They'd rebuilt trucks with engines and steering in the center for shit's sake … and in all of that, insisted on reusing an old engine? It didn't make a bit of sense, but they'd made the bed, and now people like Cutter and Abed were forced to lie in it.

"We *can't* make it," Abed argued.

"We can if I fix the problem."

"Stopping for any reason still counts as human assist. You know how the papers will spin it. And even if you work fast, we're still just barely ahead of schedule, and at this point, it's fifty hours, or you might as well—"

"I'll fix it while we're still moving."

Silence, so Cutter continued. He'd pulled a diagnostic on his tablet and was staring right at the problem. "I can do it, Abed. I've got the diagnostic right here. The oil pan gasket is leaking."

"You can't replace a gasket while the engine's running." Abed sounded deadly serious like he'd changed sides in this fight.

"Of course not. But I can seal it with nano-wax, then add more oil. That's a five-minute fix and gets us to Vegas."

More silence. Then: "You can't wax the gasket from inside the truck."

That was true. He also couldn't add oil from inside the truck. The compartment Cutter rode in wouldn't exist beyond the prototype, which would probably mean a new and fully electric engine anyway. All service considerations assumed a mechanic working from the outside, seeing as the cargo would be inside.

The oil pan was between Cutter and the road, and the oil cap was to his left at chest-level somewhere. He could see the tube emerging from the engine block and running out the side from where he stood. "I can do this, Abed."

"You're serious."

Of course, he was serious. Never before had Cutter worked on something that felt so visible, so global, and so important. He was a poor kid from Amenity, and now he had a chance to become a valid citizen like everyone else — credentialed and everything.

They'd promote him. He'd have to buy a suit. How many Dorothys back home could he help if that happened?

Cutter climbed up and popped his usual hatch, attaching the safety line to his harness. Abed saw it on his monitor.

"Cutter? No."

"Yes."

"Absolutely not. I'm taking cont—"

Cutter yanked the remote module from the engine's top. Abed banged something and swore.

"Put that back, Cutter. Plug me back in. This isn't even close to safe. Cutter? *Cutter!*"

He was already up and out. Onto the top decking, no longer caring what the drones saw. The rules of this game allowed for a technician so long as the tech was in no way a driver.

The drones knew he was there, but the AI was still in control. The test was still valid. Everyone knew someone was maintaining the trucks, just not that he was riding along. Both were okay — and would remain so, assuming Cutter could stay out of sight after this and before his papers came through.

The wind topside was far stronger than he remembered. He hadn't been out since the first few runs, back before the drones began paying attention. It took his breath away. He stopped and faced its assault, using one hand to reach back for his goggles.

His eyes stopped stinging once they were on, and by that time, his hands had accepted that they were stronger than the wind.

"CUTTER! CUTTER, GET DOWN FROM THERE!"

Moving away from the hatch, he could no longer hear the radio. This was a one-way show. Abed didn't need his remote station; he could watch Cutter's antics on the news.

They would have no idea who he was. Probably assume he was some random grease monkey. Fine, the human part of this story would vanish if he could pull this off. Or if he failed … in a long red smear on the concrete.

Cutter reached back into the trailer for his smaller tool bag, then found the tube of nano-wax. He used his teeth to bite open the sealed end, then tucked the tube between pants and skin.

The tube started working its way down his leg the second he moved. His pockets were too shallow. He'd have to carry it in his mouth, bite down, hang on tight, and pray.

The wind was a thousand angry hands, yanking him back and away. To rise too upright was to become a human sail, so he stayed low, and when he reached the ladder on the trailer's side, Cutter hugged it like a lover. The tube of wax kept slipping.

Fuck. *Oil.*

Back up the ladder. Back into the trailer.

He opened the bottle, knowing he couldn't use two hands to open it later, and repeated his descent with one hand down.

Climbing down a ladder one-handed was a complex maneuver involving handing the oil from one side to another, lacing arms through the ladder to hang on with every step.

He reached the oil fill first. The better method was to fix the leak and *then* refill the oil, but he was low on hands and options. So with the wind pulling him from his place and traffic whipping by at impossible speeds to one side, including the occasional screaming horn, Cutter squeezed the oil in one armpit and used the same hand to undo the cap.

He had nowhere to put the cap, so he pinched it between his lesser fingers and took the oil in the big fat ones, juggling both.

Oil spattered when he tried to upend the bottle. He got it into the hole with effort, chugging into the block while another honking car screamed by, full of kids, hooting and hollering.

Someone threw something, and someone else laughed. What felt like a wadded-up fast food bag struck Cutter in the side, then broke apart on the road behind.

His breath was loud in his ears. His heart was a cannon in his chest, the blast of shotguns inside his head.

As the oil bottle finished draining, the wind caught it and flapped the thing violently away, a stream of oil dancing behind it.

Cutter rushed to return the cap, but it slipped in his fingers, gone in seconds. "Fuck."

It was nearly impossible to think. He had been in tough situations, but never one that felt so close to death. People weren't meant to cling to the side of a truck shooting down the highway at over eighty miles per hour. Doing so bred a unique kind of terror — one Cutter couldn't look in the eye without going mad.

Just do the job. Just stick something — anything — in the hole. It's six hours. You can make that.

Cutter looked down and around. He had the tube of wax, assuming he didn't lose it to the wind, and the oil fill was far too big for it … and too small to shove the tube itself inside. But that was it.

So he hooked the ladder again and carefully removed a shoe. He stuck the shoe down the back of his pants, then managed to doff a sock. The sock went into the fill hole like a big Molotov cocktail.

Now the pan. Now the part that's downright insane instead of just stupid.

The ladder bent beneath the trailer, built that way because you could hinge it down while the truck was above the hopper if you needed to go lower to work the hatch. While locked in its folded position, the ladder made a nifty little set of playground rungs for crazy people.

Cutter started, then snagged. The safety line was too short.

Shit. Shitshitshitshit …

He'd come this far and gone this crazy. Cutter

unclipped the line and re-clipped it to the ladder to keep it from swinging. Maybe this was better. He'd had visions of swinging from the line like Tarzan's vine, banging against the truck's side because he couldn't find his bearings to stop it.

At least this way, he'd fall to the road, get ground flat or run over. His death would be immediate.

Go. Now. Before you lose your nerve.

The crawl under the truck was so much harder than he'd imagined. Once gravity was below his back instead of under his feet, Cutter turned out to be a good deal heavier than he'd thought and had to cling with both hands and legs for dear life. There was still a lot of wind under the truck — something the engineers should look into because eliminating the gust would improve efficiency. And finally, although there was a good two feet between him and the road while he hung horizontally under the truck, it felt like millimeters.

Cutter kept himself snugged tight — a position that required his biceps and core to flex without reprieve. He was holding himself at the midpoint of an upside-down pushup, the world's angriest belt sander waiting to flay his back.

He made his way to the pan, barely able to reach it from the locked-up ladder. Only one hand would make it, and that arm was stretched all the way out.

He hung. And stretched. And his heart cried mercy, and his lungs could barely breathe, and the blue sweat of oil smoke below wasn't helping.

It took far, far longer than expected to apply wax all the way around the pan (he didn't know which part was leaking), then climb back out. By the time he was on the truck's side again, Cutter had dropped the tube of wax and had no idea when.

His mind was screaming. There was no way to focus or think.

He stayed that way for too long. The side of the truck was far from safe, but it felt so much safer than hanging below.

More cars — more trucks, each with a bleat of the horn — screamed past.

Cutter gave himself a count, swearing he'd start moving again after just a few more seconds of rest.

Three.

Two.

One.

He climbed up. Over. Inside.

The hatch closed, and he found himself collapsed face-up on the floor of the hot and sweaty claustrophobic compartment.

Abed was yelling something inarticulate over the radio, congratulatory and angry. Then his voice stopped, and Cutter's vision swam from strange to unseeing. Beyond that, there was only the thrumming engine and the relentless rhythm of the road.

FIVE HOURS and forty-three minutes later, the truck pulled into Vegas station, drove itself over the hopper without assistance, and unloaded its freight. Cutter popped the hatch and half-stumbled out, concussed but happy.

There was champagne. Applause. Some people had made signs and banners. Cutter was surrounded, but only after a while did he know by whom. He remembered being held up like the birthday boy at a bar mitzvah. He remembered hands in his hands, shaking them. He remembered hands on his shoulders, telling him he was crazy and a goddamned hero.

Vegas to Montana to Vegas, loading and unloading without a human ever once touching the wheel.

They'd done it. V-See had made the promised run under the AI's command alone in less than fifty hours. The program would be proudly funded next month. The fleet would be improved, and the company would live on the world's map, forever grateful.

He fell asleep soundly that night.

But the next day, Cutter came to work ... and, along with half the long-haul drivers, learned that he'd been fired.

Thanks and no thanks.

The ghost had done well, but unfortunately, his services were no longer required. Unfortunately, as always, Cutter had never existed.

Chapter Six

It had to be a mistake.

He simply wasn't understanding correctly, was all. Cutter had been fired before (though it'd always been handled regrettably and called "laid off" to soften the blow, though Cutter knew a death knell when he heard one), but those situations had logic to them even if it wasn't the kind he enjoyed.

When he'd been laid off from grounds maintenance in Lafayette, it'd been because the golf course was closing, the keepers no longer needed. He was let go from the assembly line in Denver because demand had fallen; a whole wing of the company he'd worked for was shutting down. He'd lost his job three or four times because although his work was solid, it just wasn't worth the Promenade's wrath to be caught employing someone who by all social rules was clearly unemployable.

Ghosts were supposed to be for sweeping and lugging and pulling weeds — jobs that paid cash because they came and went. But this time was different. Cutter was barely a ghost with Hollander Sitwell; they'd promised him an identity. He'd been paid legit and apparently had the paper, somewhere, to prove it.

Most importantly, he wasn't in a shrinking industry, and demand for his work hadn't dropped. Quite the contrary. He was in a line of work that had just broken wide open … and most relevant of all, Cutter himself had been the one to break it.

"That's what I'm trying to explain, Mr. Dunn," said Jaxon-with-an-X's receptionist — a girl named Penny who couldn't be over nineteen and who, Cutter felt sure, Jaxon had hired mainly as set decoration. "The official record says you weren't even on that truck."

"That's insane. Check it again." And then, because he wasn't Jaxon, he added, "*Please.*"

She shrugged. "There's nothing to check. Here. Look." Penny turned her computer monitor and showed Cutter the project report. Her finger landed on the words, **PROJECT COMPLEMENT: UNMANNED.**

"But I've been on that truck for every single run since the project began."

"I'm so sorry. I don't know what to tell you."

"It's a mistake. It's clerical."

"I'll take it up with him when he's available. That's really all I can do."

Penny seemed like a nice girl. Perhaps Jaxon had beaten her into it, but either way, Cutter knew she wouldn't budge or couldn't.

He sighed. "I'll wait."

"For what?"

"Until he's free." Cutter sat, glancing at a fan of nearby magazines, seeing the latest was from three years prior.

"I'm afraid you can't do that, sir."

"Why not?"

"Mr. Bristow's request."

"I'm just sitting here." He flapped a magazine. "Sitting here reading *People*."

"I'm sorry. It's his policy."

When Cutter didn't budge, she whispered, "*He yells at me when I let people wait here*."

"Can I call him?"

"You'll get me, sir."

"And you'll put me through?"

"Well …"

"Because I can just go back to the B&B and call him right now. Those walk-around phones don't work for me because … Well, they don't work for me. But the bed and breakfast … *What?*"

It looked like she'd bitten a lemon. "I'm afraid that reservation has been canceled."

"But it's my reservation. It's where I've lived for the past six months."

"I'm sorry."

"I pay for it. *Me*. Not Jaxon-with-an-X."

"Oh, yes, sir. But it's a company property."

"Hollander Sitwell *owns my B&B?*"

"*Their* B&B. Yes, Mr. Dunn. I'm afraid that's the case. And …" Her eyes ticked away. "I've been asked to tell you that that particular housing is required for another party."

"Which other party?"

"I'm not at liberty to say."

"But you know."

Penny didn't reply.

"Who?"

"I can't say."

"Is it the Boogeyman? Bigfoot? The Tooth Fairy? The Loch Ness Monster?"

"Um …"

"Look. It's 'Penny'?"

She nodded.

"Penny, I'm all ready to work. I've got my tools in my pack. I stayed up half the night outlining changes to the design. First thing is to swap out the engines. The project's proven itself now, so it's time to get rid of the diesel and oil and do this thing right. The compartment needs to be redesigned. I figure we'll want a few more runs with a mechanic aboard, but after that, there's no sense in it, and right now, we're giving up — what? — thirty, forty square feet of space that could be filled with vanadium. I ran it by a math guy I know, and he says that just eliminating the compartment, by itself, will fully pay for a new next-gen electric engine after just the first—"

"Mr. Dunn. I'm sorry. I really am, but you can't stay here. If you want to talk to him, feel free to call. But you …" She made a frustrated, between-a-rock-and-a-hard-place sort of expression and lowered her voice again. "I'm really sorry, but … *I need this job!*"

Cutter stood. Then he turned back. He couldn't give up so easily. Maybe that's the way things were done in the real world, but Amenity was a place of pride, and that pride was like red cells to his blood.

You didn't let people take from you in Amenity. Not ever. Not ever, ever. Even if the cost of getting back what you'd lost was ten times what the missing thing was worth, you went after it anyway. To do less was to steal a person's dignity. Or even worse, his soul.

He marched over to Jaxon's door despite her protests, then pounded it with one fist.

"Mr. Bristow? Mr. Bristow! It's Cutter Dunn. I need just a minute of your time."

"Mr. Dunn …" Penny said.

"I just have a few questions. Please. Two minutes. Two questions. Then I'll leave you alone."

"Mr. Dunn, I have to ask you to leave."

"JAXON!" Cutter pounded harder. "Jaxon with an X! I know you can hear me. You owe me this much. At least you owe me an explanation!"

"Is there a problem here?" came a new voice.

Cutter looked back to see two large security guards. Penny hadn't touched the phone or anything that might be a panic button, so this had to be Jaxon. He was just sitting in there, maybe smug but probably cowering, keeping his mouth shut and calling goons to make his inexplicable problem go away.

"No problem at all. I work here. Maybe you heard of me. I'm the guy who made the Montana run possible. I'm the reason this company's about to get filthy rich." He pounded even harder on the door, now rattling the lock. "I KNOW YOU'RE IN THERE! IS THIS HOW YOU THANK ME? COME OUT HERE, YOU COWARD! COME OUT HERE AND SAY IT TO MY FACE!"

"Okay. All right, Mr. … " But the guard trailed off there.

They both wore unnecessary riot helmets. A small heads-up display was visible from where Cutter stood, and it seemed the guard had hit the end of his sentence prematurely due to insufficient information.

The man in Jaxon's office was not coming up with an identity, it seemed — not a state license, not a federal credential, not even a company ID. Most city people weren't used to seeing total blanks. No wonder their first reaction was usually fear.

While the first guard gaped and the second tapped in the air to find the same thing on his own HUD, a radio crackled. The first man listened, then came forward: orders from inside the office, it seemed.

"Let's go, Mr. Dunn," said the second man. "Time to head outside."

"So now you know? Good. Cutter Dunn. Sound familiar? Tell me. Would *you* fire me after what I did?"

"I'm sure I don't know what you mean, sir."

"The V-See run. Vegas to Montana."

"And?"

"I ran it. I was in the trailer."

"Let's go, sir."

"You don't believe me?"

"The Montana run was unmanned, sir. That was kind of the whole point."

Cutter was quickly making his way from uncomprehending to incredulous. He was a man standing under a bright blue sky while everyone around him insisted it was red.

"There was drone footage of me hanging off the truck. It was on the news when I came out in Vegas. Everyone cheered."

"That's a really nice story, sir."

"You don't believe me?"

"Let's go, sir."

Guard #2 had tried to take Cutter's arm. He wrenched away, eyes daring the guard to do that again.

"Find the celebration footage. I saw cameras. I *know* it was recorded. You'll see. It's me who comes out of the truck."

Now Guard #1 tried. Cutter punched him in the throat, and the man began gasping, grabbing his neck in a scramble to breathe.

The second guard came at him, but Cutter went instantly calm, holding up a hand.

"Just look. That's all I want. Find me the Vegas terminus. Yesterday 8pm or so. I don't want to fight. I swear I'm not trying to be unreasonable. I'll even go if he wants me gone, but not without an explanation. If the company wants to kick me to the curb after I risked my life to make the most significant advance in their history, okay. But I at least deserve to know why."

Cutter changed his tone, now looking the second guard in the eyes, not as an opponent, but just one more human being. "Please. I ... I don't understand."

It was the last thing he said before something cold and metallic shoved itself against the back of his neck. It seemed that Guard #1 had recovered unseen ... and, as it turned out, he carried a stun gun.

Chapter Seven

JUNE TURNED out to be kind of a badass. She didn't actually own the B&B. The deed belonged to Hollander Sitwell, a Nevada corporation. She *had* owned it once upon a time, but her husband (August, she told Cutter his name was, to go with June and July ... but she couldn't keep a straight face and burst out laughing) had made a string of bad investments — ironically in other bed and breakfasts — and had fallen behind.

He'd worked for HS back when they were still making decorative glass globes, and Hewlett-Packard before that, a company man through and through. He believed in safety nets and pensions. So he'd let the company buy the place and bail him out, even finding himself over the moon after they invited June to stay on and manage it.

They're holding it for us until we get back on our feet, he'd said, but the company had refused every offer to buy it back after that... and, according to June, kept raising the rent.

June wasn't hardass enough to defy the company outright, but she did give them a night's worth of the finger. She'd been told that her boarder was finished in town and should be shown to the station.

"To hell with them," she said. "The least I can do is let you pack."

Ironically, her kindness did him no favors. Cutter had marched back to the bed and breakfast with a continent-sized chip on his shoulder, stubborn Amenity blood surging like a river inside him, determined to squat where he stayed and force the place to evict him. There were laws about such things, and only so much an owner could do to remove even a temporary lodger. Cutter planned to chain himself to the radiator. Force them to call the cops on him.

June changed all that. After hearing her story and seeing her willingness to take a modicum of wrath on his behalf, he determined not to make her life difficult. She was a victim, and this was still — in spirit if not legal deed — her home. She and July lived in the private unit ... and Cutter would be damned if he'd do anything to hurt them.

So he took the night June defiantly gave him, then packed his bags. He'd go somewhere else, to a place not owned by Hollander. There were plenty of motels in town, with rooms to rent.

But he soon discovered that things wouldn't be easy.

He was on his way out for the final time when June stopped him. She took him by the arm and looked him in the eye.

"You need anything, Mr. Dunn, you let me know. Anything. My husband was like you before there were 'people like you.' He never liked eyes on him. Kept a low profile and always paid cash. The one trust he made was to the companies he worked for ... and look where that got him."

"Actually," Cutter said, "if you don't mind, there is something."

THEY WENT to the bank together. June knew how to take ducat currency, which was virtual and change it to cash, which could be rubbed between his thumbs. The process was dirt simple, she told him on the ride over. The teller should have been able to pull up his account so he could request some American green.

But Cutter ran into the same problem he'd already run into at the local motels. The entire system, from end to end, was digital. No touch required.

But of course, Cutter had no credentials, and now thanks to the Hollander Sitwell gaffe, he'd never get them. He might as well have been swiping air.

"Are you sure you have an account, dear?" June asked him as he struggled.

"Yes. Sure. I saw the papers." And there was more. Last night, before he went to sleep and after a dozen nonstop hours of harassing everyone he could find, he'd finally received a phone call from a woman identifying herself as Shoshana Lind, Esquire. And she actually said the *esquire*.

From context, Cutter took this to mean she was a lawyer. The lawyer told Cutter that the company wanted very badly to honor his work and leave him happy and content with his completed service.

This seemed to imply they also wanted to leave him *quiet*. An odd bargaining took place wherein the amount of severance offered by HS went up every time he demanded again that someone answer his questions. They finally settled on an amount that prompted no further inquiry.

There had been new papers, sent electronically to June's machine and duly printed so that Cutter, the philistine, could hold the proof in his hands.

"Cutter. Honey." June kept pacing and Cutter, self-conscious of all the time he was taking, kept telling her to go home. "I need to run out for a few—"

"Please, June. It's fine. You drove me here. You told me how to do the conversion. Nothing to it, really. Just ask for some of my money in dollars, and they'll do the rest. Right?"

Cutter could do the math in his head. The anonymous VP had told him he had fifty grand in his account, and the negotiated severance was another fifty. Ten was gone, sent to Dorothy for her medical bills.

"Easy as pie," said June. "But—"

"But nothing. I can't thank you enough, but I'll feel terrible if you get in trouble with your landlords because of me. I'm *persona non grata*. I can take a hint. I'll be gone tomorrow. I've got cash; there are plenty of places I can stay."

"You're sure."

"Of course, I'm sure."

"Then godspeed, Mr. Dunn. And may the dust be always at your feet."

It wasn't an expression Cutter had heard before, but he understood the soul of it fine.

June took his right hand in both of hers, smiled, then let him go.

CUTTER HAD to wait for nearly an hour. The banker whose turn he was waiting for kept finishing with a client, then looking at him, then puttering through the paperwork on her desk. Another client would eventually enter, and the banker would sit with them for a while.

The cycle repeated until Cutter intercepted the banker on her way to the bathroom. "Hi."

"Oh. Hello."

"Remember me? You were looking up my wallet number."

"Oh. Yes. Of course."

A pause. They stood awkwardly.

"And?" Cutter said.

"Well, there's a bit of a wrinkle."

"What kind of wrinkle?"

"I'm afraid we're not ..." More discomfort.

"Not what?" Cutter prompted.

"It's just that this is sort of a corporate bank."

"Okay."

"We deal mainly with corporations."

"That's fascinating."

"Not so much individuals. I mean, sometimes. But nothing ... specialty."

There it was. "Nobody without credentials."

"It's just that most people in your position don't use banks. We're not set up for it."

"But I have an account, right?"

"You have a *wallet*. The paperwork you gave me was actually the disburser's end of the transaction."

"What's that mean?" Cutter asked.

"Well, it had our name on it because this is where Hollander Sitwell banks. *They* sent the funds, but *your* account here ..." She squirmed.

"My account."

"You don't really have an account."

"But I have the paper."

"It's complicated. If you don't have an account, we can't access your wallet."

"But I have the wallet."

"I assume."

"So what if I *open* an account. Can you connect to my wallet then?"

"Well …"

Cutter sighed.

"It's just that this is a corporate bank."

"So I hear."

"We deal mainly with corporations."

"Sensible." He gestured around the packed lobby. "All these people are corporate reps, huh?"

"We do have some private clients."

"Great. I want to be one of them."

The banker looked trapped.

"It's because I'm uncredentialed. That about right?"

"Unfortunately, without a government ID, banking is—"

"Question for you, then."

"Okay …"

"There's money in my wallet."

"According to your papers, yes."

"You deal with money."

"Yes, but …"

"How does a 'person like me' — a lowlife, you understand — how do I *get* my money, if not through a bank?"

A half-hour later, Cutter was standing across a plexiglass partition from a man with a head so bald, Cutter kept wanting to reach out and rub it if only the stupid divider wasn't in his way. He'd already read all the rules while waiting in line, which he'd done among an assembly of folks who looked starved or high, and likely both. The place wasn't a bank so much as a moneylender of questionable legality — Cutter would pay a twenty percent commission to access his own money.

But that wasn't the worst of it. After his experience at the bank, Cutter called the motels one by one and asked about the check-in procedure. Every single one of them started check-in with an ID scan.

When he asked how they handled guests without IDs — guests with cold hard cash, mind — the conversation changed on a dime. Suddenly the clerks were no longer interested in discussing matters of habitation. Suddenly other lines were ringing, and they had somewhere else to go.

"I found your wallet and connected to it fine using your single-use third-party key," the bald man told Cutter. "No problem with that part of it."

"Great. I just need three hundred US dollars. Cash. Whatever amount of ducats that works out to."

"Well, now, *that* part's a problem," said the man.

"What part?"

"The part where you want me to give you money."

Cutter opened his mouth, but the man held up the severance transaction June had printed out, plus the original document provided by the nameless vice president that proved he'd had fifty grand to start.

"Now, look. I'm not about to call anyone on you. We all got shit going on, and God knows *I* ain't nobody's judge."

"*What?*"

"Botha these got your name on it. Same address, same temporary ID. *Worker number*, see?" He showed Cutter a swish of papers, really nothing at all. "But you fucked up."

"I don't know what you're talking about."

"Different wallet identifiers. See the problem?"

"Are you saying I have two separate wallets?"

"No, I'm saying you've got *one* wallet with two identifiers. Meaning one a'them's fraudulent."

"That's impossible. Both are from my employer."

"Yeah."

"They are!"

"Look. Like I said, I'm not gonna report it, but I sure ain't about to be party to fraud. They look at places like this first, you know."

"What places?"

"Places that work with ghosts. You think you're the only one ever come in here?" He looked around at the poverty-ridden crowd. "You people work in cash. Nothin' but cash. I pay out cash — nothin' but cash. Feds don't like cash these days. Can't trace it. Can't see where it ends up and who it pays. Cash is invisible. Like you."

"Look, I need—"

"You need to move along. Account's locked anyway."

"Locked!"

"Yeah. Happens when you mix identifiers. You want it unlocked, talk to whoever opened it for you."

Shit. That meant Hollander Sitwell. "Let me talk to the manager."

"I'm the manager. You need to go, now, or you'll be talkin' to the feds. You and your bullshit account."

"It's not bullshit!"

"Yeah."

"It's not!" Cutter exclaimed. "I just sent someone ten thousand out of it!"

"See, that right there proves it." The bald man shook one of the papers. "No matter which identifier I look at, ain't nothing come outta either'a these. Not once. Not ever. What account never gets drawn on?"

That part wasn't too strange to Cutter. He was paid on payroll in ducats, sent into an account he'd have no problem linking to once he had his credentials — and as he understood things, he should, if he wanted, also be able to get money from it before the credentials. But he was also paid a small cash stipend for his day-to-day. The only transaction — the only real withdrawal — had been for Dorothy.

"Show me," Cutter said.

"Oh, for pecker's sake. You blew it. Get out of here."

"Show me!" Cutter growled.

The man stared him down, then grunted and started typing. Then he turned the computer screen around, and Cutter saw all the exact same information ... and no transfer of ten thousand.

"This is wrong."

"Now you're just insulting me."

"It's wrong! I ... I have the receipt!"

And while the bald man protested, Cutter opened his bag and searched until he found the transaction receipt the VP's lackey had put in his hand. He pressed it flat against the plexiglass for the man to read.

"Uh-huh. Different identifier again. Look, man. I'm not asking for trouble."

"Hollander Sitwell did this. You got me?" Spittle flew from Cutter's lips onto the plexiglass. "I didn't make this transaction. *They* did. I looked it up. Someone showed me how to look it up. The transaction's legit. I found it online."

"You believe everything you see online? You're a ghost. What the fuck do you know about 'online'?"

With perfect aim, Cutter stabbed a hand through the small hole in the partition and grabbed the teller by the collar. "I found it. Now *you* find it."

The man shook him away, then stared daggers as he

considered Cutter for a long moment, then finally said, "You really believe what you're saying."

"It's the truth."

"*Something's* the truth, but it's not what you say it is. At least not from where I'm standing. Who showed you how to look it up?"

"Someone at work."

"Uh-huh. And when you looked it up … "

"Also at work."

The bald man took a few extra beats, then looked around his lobby. He moved closer to the divider and finally talked to Cutter as if they were just two men rather than vendor and customer.

"If you're telling the truth — and I ain't allowing for sure that you are," he said, his voice low, "then maybe this is where you should let it go."

"What?"

"They're seeing one thing inside the company network." The bald man nodded to the transaction report in Cutter's hand, then pointed to his computer. "But out here, I see a whole different story."

"What are you saying?"

"That if you're not lying, then someone's cooking the books."

Chapter Eight

With no cash and nowhere to stay, Cutter found himself low on options. No motel in town would accept an uncredentialed guest, and June's wasn't the only B&B owned by Hollander Sitwell. His funds had inexplicably been frozen, and June — barely an ally — would get in boiling water if he bugged her again. He was almost completely isolated. She'd kept his room for months, despite his barely ever being there. Cutter had been living inside a truck. He had no friends, acquaintances, or coworkers other than Abed, whose face he'd never seen.

How had they isolated him so fully? He'd worked with engineers and designers at the start, did his time in a few assembly lines before the whole V-See mess. He considered reaching out, but what was the point? His ideas had annoyed the engineers, though Cutter had been right (maybe *because* he'd been right), and the suits definitely wouldn't speak to him now.

He'd chatted up his fellow workers, but that was more than half a year ago, and turnover was a constant on the line. Never before had Cutter realized just how much of a shadow his footprint had been. Drone footage, but only at a distance. No interviews about the route or its eventual success.

At first, they'd tried to hide him, and in the end, they'd been smart enough to rob him of credit. Even the crowd that congratulated his arrival, in his flickering moment of joy and success, had barely seen him.

After riding under the truck and sweating through his underwear, even Cutter's true skin color was impossible to determine through the grime. That day he'd been part of the success, not its impetus. Looking back, that much was clear. *The truck* had been celebrated … and oh yeah, there'd been a guy with a wrench somewhere in there too.

He needed help, and there was, regrettably, only one possible place to ask for it. Rambling on his lonesome was easy … but this thing with Dorothy's money kept Cutter on edge. Had she gotten his money, or was her situation worse than before?

Amenity's people didn't have phones. He could try the mail, but it would take days or weeks without a reply, assuming the mailman could even figure out where Amenity was. Shipping containers in a huge field didn't have addresses like homes in a cul-de-sac. Might as well try to mail a colony of roaches and hope the carrier didn't head in with insecticide at the ready.

He ruled out Jaxon-with-an-X. Jaxon-with-an-X, it turned out, spent all his time in the office these days. The office had a back entrance where Cutter couldn't reach it, and — maybe this was new; maybe it wasn't — flew to work in a chopper. There was no way to intercept him unless Cutter planned to bring a ram to break through his office door. So, Marie, it would have to be.

But Marie wasn't any easier. She parked in a reserved spot close to the building, and word had spread that the campus guards were not to let anyone without credentials through the outer fence.

Cutter pressed the issue, and guns were drawn.

Determined, he circled the fence in a motor pool golf cart (keys in the ignition, how lucky) and eventually found an unwatched spot more than a mile away. He walked, staying low until he got close enough to see the comings and goings. That's when he ran into the other thing.

Turned out Cutter wasn't the only one casing the building that day. He'd dodged guards for no real reason because on the east side, near the V-See wing, the entire fence had been cut and opened like a cherry bomb going *boom* in an aluminum can.

A moderate crowd of angry protesters ringed the entrance.

Cutter stayed away from them, waiting. Eventually, he saw Marie leave the west building. She worked in V-See, so there must be a passage from one wing to the others, and she'd obviously known to dodge the crowd outside.

Marie was watching the mob, trying to enter her car unseen when Cutter grabbed her by the shoulder.

She leaped, turned, then grabbed her chest. "Shit. Cutter. You scared me."

"So you *do* know who I am."

"Of course I know who you are. What's that supposed to mean?"

"Jaxon won't see me."

Her head bobbed. "Yeah. That sounds like Jaxon." She peeked behind Cutter, then around. "You shouldn't be here, Cutter. Bad news."

"What's bad news?"

"Protesters. Believe me, you don't want to be seen."

"Why? What are they protesting?"

Marie seemed to war with herself. She'd already said

much more to Cutter than she was probably supposed to. "It's the drivers."

"What drivers?"

"The drivers whose jobs you made irrelevant."

Cutter eyed the mob with interest. "Maybe I should talk to them. Explain that I wasn't the one who made them irrelevant."

"Don't. That would be a very bad idea."

"Why?"

"They'll kill you, Cutter. Don't you understand? Hollander PR doesn't see things the same way that you see them."

"Because of a misunderstanding? Or something more on-purpose?"

"I-I don't know what to say."

"Say you'll get me my fucking money."

A blank stare. "What?"

"You seriously don't know?"

"I don't know, Cutter. I swear."

"My pay. It's frozen. The bank I went to" — dignity insisted he blame the bank, not a low-rent moneylender — "said my wallet numbers don't line up."

"That's not how it works. If you have the identifier and your key … "

"I understand how it's *supposed* to work. It's not. Who's fucking with me, Marie?" He had her by the shoulders, not precisely meaning to intimidate but doing it anyway. *"Who?"*

"I don't know anything about your money."

"How about cooking the books? You know anything about that?"

"Cooking the books?"

"I know they have to keep records. Where are they? Someone needs to explain this shit to me, Marie. Someone needs to tell me whether or not a transaction I sent to a girl who really needs it … Someone needs to tell me whether or not it was sent at all."

"I …" She kept looking at the protesters, a few of which had noted an argument and were looking their way. "Did you get a receipt?"

"I got a receipt."

"And it's verified?"

"Seems to depend on where you verify it. Funny thing, Marie. I did some poking around on the way here. Are you aware of the theories surrounding Hollander's operations?"

"Conspiracy bullshit. Come on, Cutter." She tugged his sleeve. "Get in the car. Let's go somewhere private."

"This is private."

"Not for long." He was looking at the protesters, too. They were marching steadily toward the car, unhurried but constant.

"They're not your friends, Cutter."

"I was fired; they were fired. Maybe I'll get a sign. March alongside them."

Marie scrambled for her keys, but Cutter grabbed them easily, spied her car's transponder among the brass and zinc, and tossed it into the weeds.

"Cutter. Oh, shit. Why did you do that?"

"Explain."

"I can't explain! I don't know what to tell you!"

"Jaxon comes to work in a helicopter. The vice presidents all have private jets. The numbers don't add up. What's your salary, Marie? And have you *verified* it?"

"Cutter, please. Come … Come into the building." She was dragging him now. "We'll go inside. I'll treat you to vending machine coffee. Just like Mom used to brew, right?"

Cutter pulled her back. The crowd was closer, now chanting about lost jobs, lost lives, lost opportunities. It didn't even make sense. The AI trucks wouldn't need drivers, but the fleet would require more mechanics. True, almost no city people knew a wrench from a calculator, but they could be taught. Cutter could have taught them.

"Please. Let me go," she said.

"I will once you explain. If not the money, then at least tell me why I was fired."

"You weren't fired. You were laid off."

He shook her. Hard.

"Okay! Fine! You were a liability!"

Cutter felt his scowl melt into something more sinister. "*Liability*. The person who guaranteed this company's future. And at great personal risk, even after the company wanted to give up. The person who solved the problem your best minds couldn't. And did it in a day because you're all living in boxes. Can't think your way out of a microchip. Is that why—?"

"YES!" Marie shouted, panicked as the crowd neared. "*Don't you understand?* It doesn't matter what you did yesterday. It only matters what you are. The media's down our throats over this. People who stopped looking at Hollander a long time ago are suddenly sniffing around again. It's like you said. People have a grudge against this company, and V-See's stirred their interest. You think people are happy that we've got a goddamn truck fleet that can work itself? This is just the beginning. Every car and truck out there is proximity chipped. Self-driving is the norm on the highways, so what happens when it's surface roads too? All with smart windshields, manufactured by yours truly."

She looked in his eyes, knew he was getting it. "Already, there's no line of sight for most driving. Cars without our technology won't be *possible* in five years; don't you see why that's a big deal? Why it's a problem? Listen to me, Cutter. Listen to me! The world doesn't want to interact anymore. The future is automation and isolation. Hollander is building its own cars already, and the patents you made possible will keep Toyota and Ford, and everyone else from using any of the tech that's about to change the game. Who wants to drive a Ford when the other traffic, chipped, can't even see it? Other cars will be obsolete. They're invisible, Cutter ... just like you!"

Liability.

It suddenly made sense. The executives could know what was coming and what it all meant, but blue-collar folks could not.

Especially ghosts: the bluest of the blue.

Not only was Cutter's uncredentialed status a problem for anyone who discovered it (*Wait ... your biggest invention came from an illegal employee?*), but so was Cutter himself. He was a man who knew too much. They'd kicked him back to the gutter, and that's where he'd stay.

"I changed my mind, Marie. Take me inside."

"Okay." She couldn't agree fast enough. "Whatever you want."

"Me and the rest of them."

Her eyes went to the protesters — all those laid-off drivers — and then they widened all the way. "You don't understand."

"Oh, I think I understand now."

"No. You don't understand. You—"

"Hey," said someone from the mob, unsure. "Is that ... I think that's the guy who came out of the first truck!"

Cutter smiled in his direction, but the smile faded immediately. That hadn't been a kind greeting. Paired with the man's expression, it was clearly more like a threat.

It seemed these people had seen him after all. They'd

been by their trucks when Cutter had rolled victoriously in, celebrating because what helped Hollander would help the rest of them. Wealthy companies grew, and growing companies needed workers.

They'd cheered Cutter because even though they might not have known the extent of what he'd done, they knew he had something to do with the truck, and for those few hours, the truck was a boon.

Not so anymore. Cutter had something to do with the truck … but today, the truck was what cost them all their jobs.

They came at him. Hard.

At first, Cutter raised both hands and tried to explain, dodging behind cars for protection while shouting his justifications. None of it made a dent. They called him sellout. They called him scab.

After that, they threw things — whatever they could find.

"I'M ON YOUR SIDE! I'M ONE OF YOU!"

But nothing. They either didn't hear, didn't believe him, or didn't care.

He spied Marie, edging toward the building, hand soon on the handle as she looked back at Cutter with a blend of sympathy and regret: *I'm sorry for what they did to you, but it's not your bed I plan to die in.*

There was shame. There was cowardice. But it didn't stop Marie from opening the door, then presumably locking it from the inside.

He tried for a few more beats, dodging bricks and scrap wood and rocks, to align himself with the people who'd been wronged by those who'd maligned him.

But then it became clearly futile, and they broke past his protections and chased Cutter as he ran.

Chapter Nine

THE PHONE at Titan Transit was answered in a way not taught in standard customer service classes. "The fuck's this?"

"Is this Gord?" Cutter asked.

"I dunno. *Who the fuck's this?*"

For a few long seconds Cutter wondered if the phone was malfunctioning, but phones weren't that complex — especially not the old rotary job he'd reassembled from a pile of recycled parts outside a small, obsolete store ironically called The Tech Depot.

Fortunately, Vegas was large; Cutter didn't have to leave town to avoid the truckers who hated him or the company that kept him blackballed. He *did* need a phone if he was to move on and move out, though — especially if he wanted to poke the bear a little — and he needed a free one, seeing as he was a non-person with no money or means of getting any.

The phone at June's B&B was a logical choice, but Cutter was reluctant to get the woman in any more trouble. So in the absence of citywide payphones and without a wireless one himself, he'd had few options. Wiring a bootleg receiver into a phone box had worked back in the day and still worked well enough now … assuming you didn't call Dial-an-Insult by accident.

Cutter glanced at Titan's number, still in his other hand on a small white slip of paper. It was plain as day, and he'd double-checked the digits back at the library. Maybe the only place left in the civilized world with phonebooks.

"It's Cutter Dunn."

"*Cutter* … Oh, hell. Of course. What's the deal? You still remember the little people while you're up there slobbering all over that company cock?"

"I'm not with Hollander anymore. They fired me."

"Easy come, easy go."

"I need your help, Gord. Something you might be interested in."

"Oh yeah, why's that?"

"Hollander fucked us both. But it's more than that. I don't think they're playing straight with *anyone*. I actually think—"

In the background, Cutter could hear him typing.

"You still there?"

"Yeah. I'm just checking your name online. There's no mention of you in any of their press releases. I thought you were big shit? Thought they put you in charge of all the wrenches-and-screwdrivers stuff."

"I was. And they did. *Did*. Past tense." Cutter could almost hear the man shrug. "And we hit our goal. We made the run with the robot truck. You saw that, right? Less than fifty hours round trip. The first fully automated load-unload run managed entirely by computer, without any human help."

"Well. Congratu-fuckin-lations."

Cutter took a moment to reconsider. He hadn't expected this sarcasm. Was the man still bitter — angry at him instead of the company that'd stolen him away? Because sure, Cutter had left Gord's employ to work for HS, but it wasn't like he'd had a choice. Gord couldn't fold space and time to make him a fully certified citizen the way HS could — or *claimed* they could, though only now did Cutter realize it wasn't going to happen and probably never could have.

"They fired me and laid off half the long-haul truckers. After all I did. After all *any of us* did. They got their automated trucks, soon they won't need drivers. They can't let anyone know I was involved seeing as I'm a ghost. In the end, loyalty didn't matter."

"*Loyalty.* I see. So this is about loyalty. Or maybe dignity. You wanna get back at them for lying and getting the union pissed at you. That about the size of it?"

"Well …"

Gord gave a phlegmy *tough-shit-hotshot* kind of snort — one with no sympathy. "So they fired you. Get over it. I seen what they had on the news. Riots. Buncha raging truckers. I get it, and I'm with it, but ain't nothin' new. The man's been fuckin' people like us since the dawn of the dollar."

"Or the ducat."

"What?"

"Gord. You sound pissed. Fine. But I need just a few minutes of your attention. Real minutes where you aren't busy being an asshole. Okay?"

It was too-straight talk, but in the past, Gord had always liked a man who said how it was.

"All right. But I got a potato in the oven. Ten minutes and I'm eating it whether you're done or not."

A pause. Apparently, Cutter had been green-lit and

should go about his business. "This isn't about being fired. Yes, I made their future, and I'll get no credit for it. Yes, I gave them all of myself, and they threw me out anyway. That sucks, but I came here with nothing, and I can leave with the same. The only reason I'm not letting it go just yet is because something keeps bugging me. Two things, but you can only really help with one."

Dorothy popped into his head, stranded without the cash he'd tried to send her — and possibly in poor health if it never arrived. But he'd done all he could on that front. He'd sent a letter. It would take time for a reply to arrive, telling him whether he was right or wrong.

Cutter considered diving into the weird money shit going down in Hollander Sitwell's pool, then decided it would only confuse things. He needed to keep things simple. Stick to what Gord already understood. "I just keep thinking about the engine."

"What engine?"

"The one in the AI truck. It was a hybrid. Not fully electric."

"*Hybrid?* You saying it ran on diesel?"

"I'm not sure. That's exactly the thing. It burned oil and fouled the spark plugs, but I can't say what it ran on. They fueled it before I pulled out of Vegas, and fueling at the mine is fully automated. The truck was a prototype. So far as engines go, it only had to run. They'll optimize it later, I suppose … but this is a company in the business, and they've got their new engines just lying around. Engines like nobody else has. But that actually seemed to be the problem: *Nobody else has them.* You deal with trucks all day, Gord. How many trucks you see with an HS-type next-gen electric motor?"

"Lots of electric trucks out there," he replied, his interest piqued.

"Yeah. But how many with HS engines?"

"None. I think they're still in development."

"The design is finished. Other trucks at HS have them. Not mine, though. Mine had a hybrid — a much older kind. And I got to thinking, *Why?* This was the most important project in the company, so why cut corners? Then in one of the meetings, I overheard someone say that there couldn't be a 'grid mismatch' if they wanted the prototype run to work. From context, I think it had something to do with the federal GPS grid. So, what's an old engine got to do with the federal grid, and why does HS act like they have access to it?"

"What's your point?"

"Hollander made smart emissions controls before they started with engines, right?"

"Yeah, sure. Pretty much nobody comes through my hub that doesn't have an HS emissions box."

"Because it's the industry standard?"

"You wanna just spit it out, Dunn?" Gord said. "I'm hungry here."

So Cutter explained his theory, though he wasn't sure yet how it all worked as a cohesive whole … if it actually did, or ever would.

Hollander Sitwell had made most of its business in glass, starting with decorative globes and moving all the way through their current domination in smart windshield technology. But the company had dabbled in other areas as well, and one of those areas was emission controls. Even though most of the current excitement surrounding Hollander Sitwell was about the company's future, those ugly little emissions boxes were where they'd made most of their money. The boxes were part of the federal environmental compliance program — and in addition to lessening harmful emissions, they also reported those emissions to the EPA for monitoring and legal reasons.

But … if the federal GPS grid had *also* been mentioned in meetings Cutter attended, and if HS's engineers wanted to make sure there was no *"mismatch"* involving that GPS grid, then that got Cutter thinking.

First, having access to the federal grid would greatly improve the chances that the AI run from Vegas to Montana and back would be successful. The grid kept track of all traffic on all roads, seeing as every vehicle legally manufactured after 2027 was GPS-chipped. There was no way to remove the chip without destroying the car because the thing was somehow distributed across many parts of the vehicle. It would be as tricky as sanding down each and every instance of a VIN.

If Hollander somehow found a way to read the GPS information for every vehicle out there, the AI running the driverless truck would have an incredible advantage, knowing when the other vehicles were changing lanes. It would know when they were speeding up or slowing down. It would know the best roads to take and when to take them. Since even driven cars were half-automatic anyway — and because drivers relied on GPS guidance more than their memories these days — it was even possible that sufficient grid access could actually *help clear the roads* as well.

The grid knew where all the vehicles were, but in emergencies, the grid was able to push new GPS info back to the cars, telling them to hold back or stay out of the way — sometimes without the drivers even noticing. This was mainly for ambulances and fire trucks. You *couldn't* drive into an emergency vehicle's path. The federal grid would know an ambulance was coming, then send signals telling the surrounding vehicles to put on the brakes or turn in another direction.

What if Hollander Sitwell somehow got access to the federal GPS grid? What if somehow, it used the emergency response function to keep the other vehicles in the AI truck's path from getting in its way?

And what would happen if *all* of Hollander Sitwell's future AI fleet could use that same cheat? Wouldn't the advantage significantly decrease shipping times and therefore increase efficiency … and set the stage for impossibly high profits?

But how to access the grid?

That was the theoretical part, but Cutter had thoughts.

What if Hollander's emission control system (which was standard and on almost every vehicle) was monitoring more than emissions? Those little boxes already sent data to the EPA, so what if they *also* picked up the GPS signal and sent *that* straight to Hollander HQ as well?

That would essentially recreate the federal grid, giving Hollander all the same traffic information and control as the feds. It would also be a gross violation of privacy, FCC regulations, and of course, federal law.

"So *why exactly* do you think they gave your truck a shitty hybrid engine instead of one of the fancy new electric ones?" Gord asked.

"Because the new engines use a next-level kind of emission controls. A new box wouldn't be a match to the emission boxes already out there. Old engines, on the other hand, still use standard boxes."

"You're saying they gave you an old engine so your emissions box would match the other boxes already out on the roads."

"Correct," Cutter said.

"And that matters because you think maybe the old emission boxes 'steal' a car's GPS signal. And send all those signals, for every car and truck, to Hollander Sitwell. *AND* Hollander can control all those vehicles the same way."

"Correct."

Gord took a moment. Cutter knew he was thinking instead of laughing in his face. Cutter wanted — *needed* — Gord to at least consider his theory. Gord sounded rough, but just because he worked with his hands didn't make him stupid. He was wicked smart in his own way, like the tinkerers in Amenity. Gord would fit right in back home.

"So you think they're cheating," he finally replied. "You think you were only able to make the run in fifty hours — without any trouble from traffic, accidents, bad drivers, or any of the other things that usually trip up AI drivers — because Hollander's little boxes stole GPS information from every car and truck around ... and cleared the way."

Cutter found himself nodding. "We didn't run into *any* trouble, Gord. Nothing that didn't have to do with the truck itself. When's the last time you took a road trip that long and ran into *zero* trouble from other cars — no slowdowns, no jackknifed semis, no nothing?"

"Rare. But it happens."

"It happened every time for me. *Every time*. The only reason I never thought it was strange was because I figured they were going out of their way to clear a path in the interest of testing. When the news reported our final run as if it were a totally realistic real-world result, that's when something started bugging me."

Gord scratched his ear, making a static sound across the phone line. "I dunno. It's a hell of a theory, Dunn. Say I buy it. Say just for a second that I'm even *willing* to buy it ... Why are you tellin' me?"

"This technology is going to shut people like you down, and if I'm right, it's not even legal."

"I don't know, man. Sure, that sucks, but I'm not looking for trouble."

"Are you looking for an *advantage*?"

The fact that Hollander was breaking the law didn't particularly trouble Cutter in and of itself, so he didn't mind letting Gord wet his beak in the same puddle if doing so could turn things around. It was the other things — the *larger* things — that Cutter was starting to suspect Hollander was up to that really bothered him. His incident at the bank, and then the loan shop, had returned his distrust of virtual currency — a realization that evoked his internal Boots, who yelled at him for ever deviating from cold, hard cash. The fact that Hollander Sitwell seemed to be twisting *that* particular titty was far more unnerving to Cutter than anything involving GPS.

But his calling Gord or doing any of this was less about idealism than survival. This was more instinctual than spite or revenge.

It wasn't on Cutter and Gord to expose Hollander, but given all Cutter had learned and his prior ties to the company, his gut said he should maybe take out some insurance. Gord was right; Cutter had been fired, and it was unfair, and that's just how the world worked. He should move on and would. But he planned to guard his back on the way. Even if Hollander never paid what they owed him — and even if they hadn't done more to Cutter so far than rob him blind and insult his dignity — Cutter would still be willing to let it go.

But he was also a ghost, and so far, the company had stolen his work and called it their own because ghosts didn't matter. And that right there begged the question: *What would happen if V-See fell into scandal over the GPS scam or the money scam that might surround it?*

Might Hollander Sitwell not turn to the ghost in their midst and use him as a scapegoat? Maybe it was paranoid, but like Boots always said: *Trust once, defend twice.* In the Amenity ethic, it was better to be prepared for an imaginary attack than to die as a fool.

"You saying you can hack their signals? Give me access to the same hijacked GPS information they're using?"

"No. I don't know anything about computers or AI. I'm not even sure what hacking is. I'm just telling you what I think might be happening."

"But you were always taking things apart."

"Sure. Toasters. Radios. Engines. I can do the kind of circuits that have actual components, not just chips. I'm good with my hands, Gord, but things need to make sense."

"What's in this for you?"

"Something they did froze a hundred thousand ducats that belong to me. I don't know if I'll ever get that money back. I don't even know if it's *real*. But that's not even the issue. I know how this probably sounds, Gord, but I need a ride. I have to get home, but I spent all of my cash a long time ago, and I can't get at anything else. The train yards up this way are too guarded for me to hitch it with a freighter. Hollander kept me in a bubble and took care of things. Now there's nothing a guy like me can do up here. I can't even enter a store without help. The doors won't open for me. So I figure I'd propose a deal. You want your business to survive, I need a way to get around, and I don't think either of us will cry if Hollander takes one in the gut. So how about this: If I'm right about this GPS thing, and if I tell you the rest of what I think might be happening and how you can take advantage, you give me one of the vehicles on your lot."

"Oh, I don't know, Dunn. I'm stretched thin as it is, and—"

"Not one of the good ones. It doesn't even need to be running, as long as it *can* run with a little time and attention. Just come here and pick me up, then let me poke around your scrapyard. I won't take anything you didn't give up on long ago."

There was a long silence on the other end of the line.

"Deal," he finally said.

Chapter Ten

FOUR DAYS LATER, after he was back to living in the small, unheated shed inside Titan's truck yard, a kid rode up on a bicycle and asked for Mr. Cutter Dunn.

"You Dunn?" The kid couldn't have been older than ten and had a dried-out, street-smart body that reminded Cutter of beef jerky.

"Yeah."

"Letter for you." He pulled something from a satchel around his neck, threaded through one armpit.

"Who sent you?"

"Corps."

"Prove it."

"I got your letter, ain't I?"

Cutter extended a hand.

"Two bucks," said the kid.

"For a letter?"

"Hey, you want cheap, get a real address."

Cutter reached into his pocket. While fixing up his future ride, Cutter had also picked up a few chores around the yard and hub, for which Gord paid him in comforting cash.

The kid and Cutter traded cash for paper with a fast snatch that looked more like a hostage swap.

As the kid pedaled away, Cutter turned the envelope over with a mix of trepidation and excitement. Four days wasn't bad time for the convoluted route of the ghosts' improvised postal service. A reply either meant great news about Dorothy and home or the opposite.

But the letter was Cutter's original. The hand marks suggested it had made its way to Amenity before being returned for reasons unknown.

He was staring at the letter, wondering what it meant and how those back home were getting on, when Gord walked up.

He looked at the truck behind where Cutter was standing with his paper enigma. It was similar to the truck on which Cutter had learned to drive when he'd been at Gord's place before, but that one was in decent shape, whereas this one was a dump. Cutter was in a rush to check on Amenity, especially now, but he couldn't in good conscience take a decent truck. Gord was a good man trying to get along, and right now, he needed anything that burned diesel without hacking.

"You get this fuckheap running?"

"Purrs like a very heavy kitten."

"No shit?" Gord frowned and half-circled the thing, touching its sides. "I figured she was terminal."

"I just have good hands, I guess."

"Yeah," Gord said. "About those hands …"

He nodded, then reached into the cab. Cutter had known he'd be coming down today and had made Gord a promise. All idealistic reasons to uncover Hollander

Sitwell's GPS fraud had vanished in a bonfire of artifice and within a minute of picking Cutter up in Vegas.

"You know, I've been thinking while I've been driving, and fuck it." Gord hadn't explained which *it* was being fucked, but Cutter knew from context and saw evidence later. Gord had already mentally added *GPS cheating* to his company's toolkit and was counting dollars. They'd know shortly if only Hollander would have that particular power.

Cutter removed a device he'd fashioned from garbage. The size of a hotplate and looked a little like one, but it served a very different function.

He turned knobs. The thing came to life with a red and a green diode (wired clumsily and taped to the side) and a low hiss of static.

"Thought you didn't do electronics?" Gord asked.

"Electronics, yes. Computers and chips are a no." He hefted the device. "This sees electromagnetic signals on key frequencies. Really no different from a twentieth-century radar detector."

"Okay."

Cutter turned the thing over. He'd mounted an oscilloscope monitor on the back. Waving lines burbled like turbulence in a brook.

"So, is it working?" Gord asked.

"I don't know. Here. Hold it."

Gord did. Then Cutter climbed up and started the truck. After all the scavenging and tweaking he'd done from Gord's well-stocked and under-appreciated junkyard, the engine hummed like it was on a showroom floor.

"Anything?" he called to Gord.

"What am I looking for?"

"Spikes."

Gord turned it and showed Cutter: no spikes. Cutter

told him how to click through the modes, got nothing, then killed the engine.

"So it's broken," Gord said.

"Maybe, but maybe not. There's not a part on that truck that's younger than fifty years. The real test is something that's not an antique."

So they tested one of the fleet trucks, which shot a spike through the oscilloscope's top. They tested another, and another, and then Gord's crapped-out station wagon, followed by the personal vehicles of every Titan employee willing to lend their keys. Even the old clunker Cutter had learned on was sending signals from both the GPS chip and the emissions box.

"So you were right," said Gord when they finished.

"I think so. I'll sister that detector to a standalone GPS unit if you have one, and—"

"I have one."

"—then we can read it and be sure."

"And then I can optimize my shipping routes?"

"You'll have the raw material, but I think you'll need a programmer to write you an algorithm if you want to do much with it."

"Good." Gord was staring lovingly at the thing, dollar signs lighting his eyes. "My nephew can probably do it."

"I'll have it for you later today."

"Then we can *really* try it out."

"Then *you* can," Cutter said. "I need to hit the road."

"Tonight? I thought we were watching football."

Cutter's hands went to his returned letter. "I need to take a rain check on that. It's time for me to ramble."

"*Ramble.*"

"It was my grandfather's word."

"You know what?" Gord looked him over from head to toe. "It suits you."

. . .

"HEY, FUCKNUT!" Gord said later, yelling from the depot's easternmost loading dock like a schoolmarm ringing the attendance bell. "Phone for you."

Cutter entered to find Gord back behind his desk — a hollowed-out space in the middle of a massive papers-and-snack-food-boxes horde. He squeezed by. The phone was a corded black thing not unlike the Frankenstein phone he'd reassembled outside The Tech Depot in Vegas. Gord had credentials and was part of the system, but otherwise, he lived a century behind the world.

The phone was off-hook, the receiver and its curling black wire flat on the desktop like a concussed snake.

"Make it quick. I got payroll to pay."

"Who is it?"

"Fuck if I know."

Gord shuffled out. Cutter closed the door most of the way, then put the receiver to his mouth and ear.

"This is Cutter Dunn."

"Can't stick to your own business, can you, Cutter Dunn?"

"Who is this?"

"Your mother."

It was a man's voice. Pretty sure it wasn't Cutter's late mother. "How did you get this number?"

"You know what GPS does, Dunn? It shows you where things are. Not really firing on all cylinders over there, are you? You sent up like ten pips. I just called the closest phone."

Cutter felt inexplicably cold. He had to mean the engines they'd just tested using his oscilloscope device. Somehow Cutter hadn't just located the signals; he'd also sent a location to himself. It made sense, but the response in itself felt fishy. The caller had to be someone from Hollander Sitwell, and the tone — down to its taunting anonymity — wasn't good.

"Who the fuck is this?" Cutter repeated.

"What are you doing down there, with all those cars and trucks?"

"Is this … Is this Jaxon?"

"Never mind who this is."

"Jaxon-with-an-X?"

"I think I can make this easy," said Jaxon-with-an-X, clearly annoyed. "I don't even need to be rude about it. I know you had some trouble getting your salary from the bank. But that wasn't on purpose. You—"

"I just sort of accidentally revealed to them that Hollander Sitwell is … what … keeping a double set of books?"

Silence. Then: "What?"

"The numbers I was given inside the company network are different from the numbers I got outside."

"Why were you comparing numbers? We gave you all you needed."

This had begun as an annoyance, progressed to a plan, and only now felt actually dangerous. The coldness in Jaxon's voice was apparent across the phone line. His tone suggested that he hadn't known about Cutter's discovery … and was quite unhappy about it.

So he wouldn't tell Jaxon that June had printed his balance. Seemed he was supposed to get that money using only the bullshit numbers instead of the real ones.

"They told me it was just a glitch. I don't really know what any of it means." The executives thought their blue-collar workers were dumb, so Cutter fed right into it.

"What are you doing with the GPS spikes?"

"Just playing around. No reason."

"Bullshit," Jaxon said.

"Fine. I just noticed something. And with time to kill, I got curious." Then, because Cutter, like the Gambler, knew when to hold them and when to fold them, he told Jaxon exactly what he thought was happening, then finished with, "Not that I care. You say you can unfreeze my money?"

"Yes."

Really selling it, he added, "And maybe it's worth a little extra. Then maybe I really don't care about what you're doing."

"How much extra?"

"A hundred thousand."

"Thirty."

"Seventy."

"Fifty."

"Forty," said Jaxon. "Take it or leave it."

Cutter paused just long enough to feign consideration. "Deal."

"Fine. Give me two days."

"Now." Cutter was thinking of Amenity.

His truck was done, and he could head out before the hour was done with him, but he'd been log-jammed on what exactly he'd do once there. If there was indeed trouble with Dorothy and if the faceless VP hadn't sent her any money — something Cutter was increasingly sure of — he'd still need cash upon arrival to solve her problem.

"Two days. I'm not the fucking bank. I don't make the rules."

"Two days," Cutter repeated. He'd have to improvise until then.

"How do I know you won't open your mouth anyway?"

"I'm an Amenity man. My word is my bond."

SEAN PLATT & JOHNNY B. TRUANT

There was a long silence as if those words actually meant something to Jaxon. But then there was a click, and the line went dead.

BY THE TIME Gord was back in the office, Cutter had a terrible feeling.

"Who farted?" Gord asked.

"I need to borrow your car."

"You have the truck."

"I need something faster. Something lighter. I'll bring it back, I promise."

"No."

"Yes."

"What, you think you can just say the opposite and convince me?"

"What I told you is worth more than your goddamn car. The *truck* is worth more than your car."

"I said no."

"OH, JUST SAY YES ALREADY!"

Gord's hair would have been blown back if he had some. "It your lady?"

"I don't know. My letter came back unopened. That call was from someone at Hollander. They know I figured out their little GPS hustle and aren't too happy about it."

Cutter didn't add that in a fit of braggadocio, he'd felt the extremely ill-advised need to boast about the other thing he knew as well, and this to a company whose history repeatedly proved just how little it gave a shit about the little guy. Boots had constantly told Cutter that if he was good to the world, the world would be good to him. The truth felt less accommodating.

"You're serious about this."

"I just need to know she's okay." Only after uttering the

words did Cutter realize how deeply he meant them, and the truth caught him by surprise.

Dorothy had always been a friend, but even though they were both unattached (the father of her baby was a one-off and had already hit the road) and otherwise compatible, there'd never been anything between them. Yet his concern now felt more like compulsion: the drive of a man to protect his wife.

Cutter didn't think he secretly loved her, but ever since first hearing news of her troubled pregnancy, Dorothy had seldom left his mind. Maybe it was that she represented Amenity. Up until Boots had made Cutter promise to see the world, Amenity was all he'd ever known. Leaving his community had shown Cutter just how much was out there … but at the same time, it'd given him perspective to see how special his own people were.

Cutter had lived among the outsiders for over half a year but had never been a part of their world … and now that he thought about it, he didn't really want to be. There was nobility in his poverty. There was honor and wonder and something special in a life with so little, where you were forced to use what God gave you: the land, the plants, and the abundant garbage freely provided by others, where a proper use could always be found.

Maybe Dorothy was the one piece of Amenity that Cutter could still put a face to. Maybe that's why she mattered so much. Or maybe it was her baby: a symbolic promise of Amenity's future and the continuation of the disconnected, ghostly way of life.

Either way, in the moment, finding her and making sure she was okay mattered more than anything else in the world.

He could think again after seeing Dorothy … and after thinking, he'd already decided he'd stay far, far away from

Hollander Sitwell and their mines full of secrets. It didn't matter that they'd hired, used, and fired him. It didn't matter that they'd done the same to half their driver fleet and would soon do the same to the rest; just in the past few days, the news said HS had spooled up every 3-D printer in its possession and was making AI trucks exactly like the one Cutter had so recently pioneered.

They could build three complete vehicles per day because robots — machines making machines — did all the work. But that didn't matter to Cutter anymore either, nor the fact that those honest-working, displaced drivers felt he was the problem.

Whatever financial scam the company was pulling, Cutter no longer cared. Even his own money (the frozen cache, plus the forty thousand promised by Jaxon) was moot.

Cutter just wanted to go back to Amenity and forget all of this. Jaxon's concerns were pointless; Cutter Dunn had no revenge in him for things that mattered so little. He was no threat to them. Boots had been right. It'd been important to try his hand in the wider world, but Boots was equally right that Amenity was still the best place for people like them.

He'd go home, start a small repair shop, and live until he was an old man … Dorothy and her baby nearby, if not literally at his side.

"All right," said Gord, dangling keys. "But I want it back. And Cutter."

He looked up.

"Be quick." Gord nodded to the now-silent phone. "Wasn't just your man who called. Gives me the creeps, the way that thing's been ringin' all day."

Chapter Eleven

CUTTER CRANKED THE ENGINE, rolled down the window, and hit the road.

Only once underway did a simple oversight dawn on him: he'd never done anything like this before. He'd grown up driving refurbished golf carts. He'd ridden endless times inside Hollander trucks, and on Gord's lot, he'd learned to operate a semi. But not once had he sat behind the wheel of a sedan and let 'er rip on the open road, with his music blasting above the wind. It was a singularly unique situation.

Cutter was almost enjoying himself when he saw the shapes in his rearview.

The sun dipped behind a cloud. He clicked off the music, superstitious somehow, and listened to the howling wind. The car was manual, and it meandered toward the shoulder if he moved his hands from the wheel. He corrected for the drift, then slung an arm over the passenger seat and turned around to look backward and noticed two things.

The first was that the three lanes of southbound traffic

were occupied to his rear by three huge rectangles riding abreast. It was like being slowly overtaken by moving boxes.

The second was that there was nothing on the road between Cutter and the boxes. And, come to think of it, nothing to the front when he turned back around. No traffic in the northbound lane, not ahead or behind.

And that was strange. But now that Cutter thought back, he was starting to believe it'd been a while since he'd seen *any* other traffic.

Quite a while, really, since he'd spied even one other car.

The realization sent a chill rippling through him.

On the forward horizon — not in the northbound lanes but directly ahead in the southbound ones — another three boxes slowly appeared.

Shit. He didn't even know why *shit*, but *shit* indeed.

There were some things that were wrong no matter where you grew up or what language you spoke, and an empty highway surrounded by enormous boxes was one of them. Cutter didn't need to know what was happening to be clear that this shouldn't be happening.

His head swiveled around. There were no exits here or place to pull off beyond the berm. His heart ticked faster.

He rolled up the window to silence the wind, so he could speak. His foot married the accelerator.

The boxes weren't boxes. He could see them plainly now, understanding why he didn't recognize them as trac-tor-trailer rigs at first. The reason was simple: there was no tractor, only trailers.

Trailers with the engine in the middle, drive wheels toward the center, and passive wheels at front and back. Giant rechargeable batteries to run the electric half of the engine, visible on the surfaces coming right at him. Six trucks, it seemed, that Hollander Sitwell had managed to spawn with a snap of their corporate fingers.

And they were coming right at him.

Think. Think think think …

But what was there to think? He had his backpack full of meager belongings, a passenger footwell stacked with empty fast-food containers, and Gord's latest load of scrapyard bullshit in the trunk.

Pull off, he thought.

But what if this was nothing? His hands were clammy, and his neck hairs were prickling, and the sun might as well be hiding for all the clear *wrongness* of right now, but the situation was simple: one car and six trucks. It might be a normal route. They might be going about their business. Probably were.

But then the first of them pulled alongside from the rear. It had happened wicked fast, and on quick inspection, Cutter saw why. The batteries mounted to the front and rear of the trucks were larger than they'd been, and the engines were so quiet, he hadn't seen them coming. They were out of the prototype stage, making new models hand-over-fist with their top-end electric engines. Must've solved the GPS issue, at least. Good for them.

A second truck pulled up on his left. Cutter had one on each side and one right behind. The three ahead were closer now, but the fact that he couldn't tell which way they were going (faced forward and slowing down or driving right at him?) was as disturbing as a man with no face.

The truck on the right boomed an enormous voice: "MERGING. MERGING."

It inched in. Cutter steered away to avoid it until the truck on his other side said, "WARNING. YOU ARE APPROACHING UNSAFE DISTANCE."

Cutter accelerated and quickly hit top end. Gord's shit-heap had a joke of an engine, compared to the silent behemoths around him.

Within seconds, the trucks closed the gap behind him. The ones ahead seemed to be facing ahead and slowing until Cutter was boxed in.

"WARNING. DO NOT TAILGATE," said the truck directly ahead.

"WARNING. YOU ARE FOLLOWING AT AN UNSAFE DISTANCE," boomed another.

There was a crunch as the right-side truck struck Gord's vehicle.

Cutter swerved, destined for a skid, but he rebounded off the left-side truck before losing control. They each moved closer until there was no distance at all.

Then they squeezed, each truck trying to merge with the space between them. The side windows shattered into tiny safety cubes. The steel members buckled. The windshield, no longer true to the shape between the bent members, popped out on one side, webbing with cracks.

"FUCKING BACK OFF! GET OFF OF ME!"

But Cutter was shouting in the dark. The trucks were drones. He was about to get smashed to death by his own creation, and the tragedy was that it seemed to be taking Hollander no effort at all.

Six months Cutter had worked on the project, and even with rapid fabrication and industrial materials printing at the team's disposal, he'd still ended up in a diesel-reeking truck missing a half-year of his life. Now that the company knew what to build, it'd been a simple matter of telling the printers what to make, the robots what to assemble, and the welding machines which joints to put together.

A crunch from the rear as he was jolted forward, colliding with the truck ahead. Both sets of batteries, behind and in front, rained bright white sparks. But neither truck slowed. Cutter could see the remaining vehicles ahead and to the sides of the diamond shape crushing him as if awaiting their turn.

Think. Think, Cutter.

What options did he have? He had nothing. Only his backpack and …

!!!

… and Gord's latest load of scrapyard junk.

Moving quickly, Cutter dove into the backseat. He needed neither the pedal nor the wheel now; the trucks provided both momentum and steering. A small peg released a lock between Gord's backseat and trunk — a good feature for a man who often transported long steel and lumber — and once lowered, he found himself facing a bounty.

But what to do with it? It wasn't like he could build a radio or a locator or even an improvised bomb, which Cutter was betting he could manage if he had the time and a rasp to grind the metal to constituent powders. He'd have to think faster. Easier. The more dead-simple his innovation, the better.

Then he had it. He began grabbing the smaller parts, ideally with a hole somewhere along their bodies. Some he had to unscrew by hand; luckily, they'd rusted nearly free. Then, once he had a double handful of small, sharp parts, Cutter removed the drawstring from his hoodie and threaded the parts into an unfastened necklace. He used the drawstring from a pair of sweatpants in the rear footwell to fashion a second necklace.

Two strings of deadly jacks held together in a line.

Working fast, unsure what the trucks had in mind if anything, Cutter bit the strings of shrapnel between his teeth and clambered forward again, punching the undone windshield out far enough to make a hole.

Then he climbed out into the curiously calm center of the truck huddle, onto the hood of Gord's car, then onto its roof.

What's this remind you of, Cutter? Huh? Huh? chanted a hectoring internal voice. *It didn't kill you last time when you climbed onto a moving vehicle, so maybe the second time's a charm.*

He'd suffered nightmares about his time dangling above the road to repair that first truck, secretly vowing to never so much as stick an arm out an open window. Now the fear was back and waging war in his head.

Only it was different now — safer yet far more dangerous. He stood at the bottom of a pixelated O — it technically had corners, and for that reason, the only wind was high up like a stratospheric flow.

Things were calm down here.

Almost as if he was safe inside a box with no top on.

But of course, if Cutter slipped now, he wouldn't hit the road; he'd be pinched between truck and car. There were no ladders; they seemed to have changed that part of the design. But, by standing on the roof of Gord's car, he wasn't so far below the tops of the truck if he jumped for it.

Wait. Not yet, dummy.

Cutter reached through the windshield, grabbed his backpack, and put it on. If nothing else, he could use the padding.

Okay. Okay. Now just take a moment to breathe. Don't jump. Don't jump. Don't—

Cowards. Twin senses warred inside but listening to either one would be folly. If he hesitated another second, he'd hesitate ten more. Then sixty, for a full minute. Then forever, until he was dead.

So Cutter leaped. His hands easily reached the top lip of the truck, but there was nothing up there to hold onto. One hand made it, but the other slipped. After a precarious moment, Cutter managed to swing the second hand up. A single heave rotated one elbow high, and a second one — this time with scrambling feet — brought the second elbow up.

From there, he was able to press upward into a powerful wind that forced him back down. Not that he'd want to be tall for what came next.

Cutter scooted forward along the truck's roof until he was at its front edge. The car, increasingly crushed like a salvage yard cube, was low to his right. Dangling necklaces of shrapnel were still in his teeth, scraping the trailer top.

He hung one of them forward, ahead of the truck's leading edge.

Wait. Just give me a second.

But there was no waiting. Cutter didn't have a clue what would happen when he did this next thing, but paralysis was a death sentence.

Please …

He dropped the string of jagged metal pieces. It clacked off the battery array, then wedged a corner of one of the pieces in a seam and stayed there.

"Motherfucker!"

It was hard to breathe up here. The wind pushed his breath back into his throat like a sock in his windpipe. He had to turn away to inhale, then squint his eyes into slits. He had one shot left.

And again he thought, *Please*.

He tossed the string forward in a gentle arc, giving the thing just enough momentum to outstrip the wind. It barely cleared the battery, landing on the concrete road, bouncing once before disappearing beneath.

Time slowed. The millisecond after it vanished wasn't even a blink, but Cutter was sure that the tridents had gone right between the big rig's wheels.

The first tire shredded. And the second, right next to it.

Then a *THUP* and a *SQUEAL* from the rear tires.

Four tires were thundering and popping, the whole rig jittering like an amusement park ride. Shards of black rubber flew upward and at deadly speed.

A second later, the rig began to sway. It slowed, losing pace with its brothers. There was a sickening scream of sundering metal as the semi's compacted side broke away from the car's wrinkles and fell back.

It swerved, the center-mounted drive wheels spinning under the AI command as the whole thing tried to regain control.

Cutter hung on, eyes closed and face pressed to metal, just trying to survive. The shredding sounds stopped, and the whole thing fell a few degrees to the right, throwing sparks and screaming like tortured demons as the rims struck blacktop.

It fishtailed toward the berm, onto the shoulder, into the dusty roadside.

Balance shifted, then recovered.

His hold stuttered as he waited for the thing to lose its balance.

It held. And then, as quickly as the whole debacle had begun, it was over.

Cutter climbed down. The drive wheels were still spinning in the dust. Like a beetle turned upside down.

He went to the front, where a small glass housing concealed the cameras and sensors that comprised the truck's electronic eyes — the front brain where the AI lived.

He couldn't kill the AI. No point in bothering. But he could smash the smart glass of the miniature windshield and catch its pieces in a ball cap from his bag.

He wrapped the glass-filled hat in a T-shirt, then stuffed it upright in his backpack to keep it from spilling.

He heard tires squeal behind him as the other five trucks, through intelligence unknown to Cutter, somehow realized that they'd lost their prey.

He didn't give them time to zero in if they were even able.

Instead, he ran and ran.

Chapter Twelve

ACROSS THREE MILES of unincorporated land was a smaller, less-traveled road. Several normal, driver-driven trucks huddled around a greasy spoon near the next stop on the freeway. Cutter went to the first of them, staying low, and searched through the unlocked toolbox mounted to the outside.

Inside was a tube of all-purpose adhesive. He took it, walked three steps away, then turned back and rummaged through his bag until he found a small video toy he'd picked up and meant to bring back for one of the Amenity kids. He dropped it in the toolbox. He wasn't sure if the driver would want it, but leaving a trade felt better than stealing.

He uncorked the adhesive, then used it to smear the entire inside of the ballcap. This done, Cutter returned the glass to the hat, moving the pieces around until they covered the interior surface. When the thing was dry, Cutter had to open it a few sizes to put it on his head. He verified in a truck mirror that he looked socially idiotic but not actually suspicious, then waited outside the restaurant's entrance, entering very close to the man in front of him.

There was a small screen to the door's right, advertising cigarettes. As the man and then Cutter passed, the display said,

"Hello, Mr. Dooley. Wouldn't you like a Marlboro today?

"Hello, Mr. Dooley. Wouldn't you like a Marlboro today?"

The man in front of Cutter — Dooley, apparently — looked at the screen, muttered something about bit and pixels and how the thing could go fuck its mother twice and moved away without looking back.

Cutter waited until the man was out of earshot and moved close again to the screen.

"Hello, Mr. Dooley. Wouldn't you like a Marlboro today?"

Cutter touched his hat full of smart glass as if encouraging this to work. "Yes. I'd like a Marlboro."

"How many would you like, Mr. Dooley?"

"Just one."

"Your price is two ducats. Confirm?"

"Confirm."

There was a chugging sound as a single cigarette dropped into a tray, charged presumably to Mr. Dooley. Hard to believe it'd actually worked, but this was another of Hollander's known issues, the possibility of short-term identity cloning perfectly obvious to the company but ignored until a scandal forced their hand because fixing things was often expensive.

He held up the cigarette. Two ducats. For one. He assumed it'd meant a pack.

Cutter walked toward the back, where a phone was mounted. That was the strange thing about truckers: they often actively didn't *want* a tether to home. It'd become a career for the professionally nomadic — people who weren't unregistered like Cutter, but half wished they were. Their obsession was his gain because once everyone stopped carrying cell phones, public phones — at least at truck stops — had made a comeback.

He stopped by Mr. Dooley's table, faked picking the cigarette up off the floor, and then said, "Did you drop this?"

Dooley, seemingly a smoker, didn't think this was strange at all. "Shit. Fuckers just roll everywhere, don't they?"

The phone's display came up: DOOLEY, PHILIP. SUFFICIENT BALANCE. DIAL WHEN READY. LONG-DISTANCE CHARGES APPLY.

Well, there was nothing Cutter could do about that. He didn't have money to pay Dooley for his phone call, so he'd just have to make it quick.

Instead of dialing, Cutter pulled up the touchscreen and navigated until he found the number for Cajun Junction Hospital.

"Cajun General," said the operator.

"Hi. I'm looking for an orderly who used to work there. I'm not sure if he's still there. It's been a few years."

"What's your party's name, sir?"

"Khalif Ramad."

"Hold, please."

Time clicked away. Cutter tried not to get his hopes up. Khalif had only come through Amenity briefly, though a lot of folks had wanted him to stay. Khalif had credentials — a bona fide citizen — unlike everyone else in the settlement. So it'd made no sense to stay, though he hadn't gone far and had stayed a friend ever since. But it'd been a while — a year or two, maybe more. It was Khalif who (if

Cutter's money made it home) would ideally make sure Dorothy got what she needed.

The phone began to ring. A thick, deep voice answered. "This is Khalif."

"Khalif. My name is Cutter. Cutter Dunn. I don't suppose you remember—"

"Cutter! Fuck you, like I'd forget! Your man was Boots. He made his own whiskey. Right?"

The thought of Boots was bittersweet, but a smile came to his face anyway. "That's absolutely right."

"How are you, man?"

"I'll be honest. A little rough. Look. Do you know if anyone from Amenity came through recently? A pregnant woman?"

"Who?"

"Dorothy Malko. Do you know her?"

"I don't know her. Want me to ask around?"

Cutter shook his head for nobody. As much as he wanted to know what'd happened with Dorothy, there was little use in it now.

"Yes. Please. But after we're done. I … I know how this must look, but I could really use some help."

Now Khalif sounded concerned. "Yeah, man, of course. Anything for my people. I've been sort of worried."

Alarm bells. "Worried? Why?"

"Lot of people sniffing around out there. I'm sure they have it handled, but you know how it is. Better to lay low. I remember nobody ever *wanted* attention."

They talked for twenty minutes. Khalif told Cutter what he'd heard, and Cutter unloaded on Khalif as if he was his brother instead of a random nomad he'd known long ago for the length of one summer. There wasn't much more to hear about Amenity; it was just as he'd said:

government chatter about cleanup and ghost profiling, same as happened now and then regardless.

But Khalif was supremely bothered by Cutter's story. After the story about what happened with the trucks, the same theory Cutter had delivered to Gord suddenly sounded a lot more plausible.

Not only was Hollander Sitwell up to no good, but they were also at least tacitly homicidal. It was possible, maybe, in a bizarro universe, that the trucks had malfunctioned when they tried to run Cutter down, but even if that's all it was — even if somehow, nobody had sent them — it was pretty bad. GPS fraud and financial shenanigans were plenty plausible for a group like that.

"Don't tell anyone else. And ..." Cutter sighed. "And definitely don't do it over the phone. This is AI we're talking about. Who knows — maybe it can listen in."

"We're on the phone right now, bud."

Cutter sighed again. "I need someone else to know. I was going to let it go, but now I think I need to run. I'm headed your way. I just get this feeling. About Dorothy. About all of them."

"You think she's hurt? Because buddy, even if your money didn't go through, I can get them to admit her on the basis of—"

"I don't know. I'm ..." Cutter sighed again. "Look. I'm sorry I called."

"No, man, no. I'm glad."

"I don't know many people with phones. You're pretty much the only credentialed person I know at all whose favors I haven't exhausted or who I'm not worried might try to kill me." He was about to add, *I know how unnecessarily dramatic that sounds,* but the truth was he'd been nearly pancaked by six robot trucks, and that was a pull-the-panic-cord situation if ever there was one.

"Okay. First, fuck off. I told you. Amenity to the end. I'm one of you, not them, brother. I sneak shit out all the time and send it over. You know Angel Industries with the care packages? That's me."

"That's *you*?"

"Course it's me, shitbird! So listen. If you hadn't called me, I'd have kicked you in the balls. Really fucking hard. So don't you bitch out on me now. You want help? You wanna get back at them? I'm your man."

Cutter exhaled, relieved despite his pride.

"Okay. Okay, thank you. But I don't want to 'get back' at anyone. I just want to get out. They're serious. Really, really serious. You know ghosts, Khalif. We don't need to 'win.' We don't even *want* to win. All that matters is to stay hidden. To survive. Once I've got that, then okay, I'll blow the whistle. Send an anonymous package to the feds or something. But until then—"

"Sure, man, sure." Something jangled. "Where you at? I'm coming to get you."

"What? No. Thank you, but you've got a job. You—"

"Fuck you, man!" he blurted, sarcastic but also serious. "You deaf? I said I'm helping, and help I'm gonna. I don't guess you can send me a ping?"

"GPS is the last thing I want to send. I'll just be happy if nobody's listening in on this call."

"Okay, then describe it."

Cutter did, to the best of his ability. He gave Khalif the name of the restaurant, the route number, and the interstate exit he seemed to see from where he was standing. And while he stood there, though it almost had to be his imagination, Cutter swore he saw another faceless truck screaming by.

"Cutter? You still there, bro?"

"Yeah. Yeah, I'm still here."

"Half hour. Maybe forty-five minutes. You hang tight."

"Sure. Thanks, Khalif."

Cutter went outside, feeling watched. Wondering if he was paranoid or if he'd been stupid to make a phone call … one in which he'd said that *yes*, he sure would like to blow a whistle.

But it was crazy to worry about that kind of thing …

Chapter Thirteen

KHALIF WAS FIVE-SIX, slicked-back hair, built like a fireplug. He worked out but was mostly just made that way. He'd grown thicker around the middle than the last time Cutter had seen him but was otherwise the same old man. Being in the car with him was a lot more comforting than Cutter, who usually prided himself on being his own man, liked to admit. Khalif, though not really from or part of Amenity in the usual sense, was still kin to it — the closest to home that Cutter had seen in a long time.

Only on the heels of that thought did it strike Cutter just how homesick he was. How lonely. Boots had always painted a romantic picture of his rambling days: One man, on the rails with nobody else and not a care in the world, taking in the sights and getting his hands dirty. The reality for Cutter had been far more existentially daunting. Rather than feeling romantic, being on his own had felt ... well ... *lonely*. He'd felt restricted, not free. His options were few because he had no one to count on. He needed people, and his reluctant humility had been ground down far enough by now that he could admit that, *yes*, people needed him.

His place was not out here. The wider world valued a ghost's manual abilities, but only so much. These weren't his people. They weren't honest, the way Boots led him to believe. Or at least, the endgame had proven a lie. His travels before Hollander were okay — charming, even — but now the taste in his mouth made him want to spit and be done with it.

He'd do as he'd told Khalif, though he probably shouldn't have said so over the phone: he'd lay low, then find a way to expose HS for all they'd done wrong without revealing his participation. There was proof out there if he looked, and he could collect it without risking his neck. Cutter knew how and what he wanted. Most of all, he understood that the frenzied, heart-pounding intensity of everything would vanish the first time he confirmed Dorothy was fine.

Or really, even if she *wasn't*, though he didn't like to think about that. What would be the very worst? That she had died? It would crush him, but right now, ignorance and negative anticipation haunted him more than anything.

"Look, man," Khalif said after a half-hour of driving together. "I'm just saying."

Cutter didn't really know, hear, or care what he was saying. He liked Khalif a lot, but the man was white noise … and he suspected Khalif took no offense if he barely listened. There'd been no trucks on the road, and because of it, Cutter had settled until he could almost relax.

His head was against the headrest; his eyes kept sighing closed; he could almost go to sleep. He wanted Khalif to keep talking, even if it was all inanities. It was the soporific drone of a conversation.

"You hear me, Cutter?" It seemed this time, he actually wanted an answer.

His eyes opened the rest of the way. He turned his head without sitting up. They were closer now; Cutter recognized landmarks he'd known all his life. Amenity wasn't far. Beyond the set of double highways was the vast tract that the shipping company owned but nobody tended. They disposed of containers, and the ghosts moved in. The best kind of synergy.

"Yeah. I hear you."

"So what about it?"

"What about what?"

"Well, don't you think they're skimming?"

Cutter yawned. He hadn't realized how tired he was before now. The adrenaline high of his deadly truck adventure had dissolved into a haze that felt like a lie. He hadn't done any of that; of course, he hadn't. Who was attacked by trucks? Cutter had seen a movie about it. People trapped in a truck stop. It had been abjectly terrible.

"Who?"

"The company."

"Oh. Sure. Skimming."

"Cutting corners here. Cutting corners there. Man, I tell you." He didn't volunteer what specifically he was telling. "I see it at the hospital all the time. The system gives a budget to the director. I don't know what the fuck. Say a million. Because whatever, but say it's like a million ducats a year. To keep the numbers simple. You know."

"Uh-huh."

"If the hospital doesn't spend all its money, the system lowers the total for next year because they figure our hospital doesn't need a full amount. So the director, he rigs it. And I know, you see the thing where they'll use the money in ways that make sense like they'll buy computers for everyone or a new copier or chairs or whatever. But our guy?" Khalif shook his head. "Cheap prick. *Criminal* prick. He's in with the drug reps. And he'll buy, like, all the pharma they've got, to max out his million or whatever. Then when the year passes, they let him refund it, minus a little. You know. Like, they keep some as a kickback, and they put the rest back in the account, then our boss has all these free lunches and a company car and stuff. He can't just take the cash, but it's as-good-as. So I get it, that's probably what your pricks are doing."

"I don't know, Khalif."

He slammed his hand on the dashboard, making Cutter jump and eliminating every trace of fatigue. He startled, nearly hitting his head on the windshield.

"MAN! That's what's wrong with this country." Khalif stabbed a finger into the center console like snubbing out a cigarette. "That right there. Greedy fuckers, man. Capitalism at its worst. So that's why I'm saying. We need to do something. Call them on it."

"I hear you, but they just tried to kill me."

"Maybe, man. Or maybe it's just one more case of not paying attention. They got bad code. What are they going to do about it? Sloppy."

"I don't think it's bad code. But yeah. They're sloppy."

Cutter told Khalif about the thing with the hybrid engines instead of the new electrics, but this time used it as an example of cutting corners and being cheap. Then he remembered something else, now that he was fully awake.

"Here's something else. They use GPS to figure out where all the other traffic and everything is, but their own system is proprietary. It navigates based on their shipping checkpoints. And, okay. Makes sense. But it's not future-proof. Every time a checkpoint moves, they have to write a patch. It's too far gone to change everything over to really using GPS for internal uses, but they say this way is more accurate, and it does make integration with their other systems easier from what I understand, not being a software guy."

He shrugged and continued. "Everything's based on Vegas. Every point is X number of miles, feet, and inches from Vegas in Y compass bearing. It sits on top of the global positioning map but isn't actually the map. I told them they should do it all over before we got started because if their headquarters ever moves, and they can't use their Vegas location as a reference anymore, their map would break."

"So you think they're doing like my hospital story?" Khalif asked. "Skimming money the stockholders want spent on legit shift and keeping it for themselves?"

Cutter nodded. He didn't exactly know how, but something was definitely going on. Internally, company money was being spent one way. Externally — publicly — it was spent another. The entire system of ducat currency was supposed to make that impossible because of unique identifier keys and federally audited paperwork kept as hard copies and all sorts of technical reasons Cutter didn't care to understand.

But impossible or not, Hollander was clearly up to something. The highest-up people were paid more than they were officially compensated; other programs were likely robbed blind a bit at a time.

It was all a drop in the bucket — and far too much for a guy like Cutter to involve himself in. He was free now and almost home.

Forget Hollander Sitwell. They'd won; he'd lost. But that was just fine, seeing as he'd never have to think on them again.

"Hang on," said Khalif. "What's this horse shit?"

At first, Cutter thought he was spinning more yarns, but then he looked up and saw that the road was blocked by two police SUVs and a mess of white-and-yellow sawhorses with construction lights on the top.

"This can't be for you, right?" Khalif said.

"How could it be for me?"

"Dunno, man. You're the paranoid one. You're the one's being all secretive and running."

Of course, that's not what it was, but nerves made him slouch down. It wouldn't have mattered; Khalif pulled up to the blockade a minute later, then there was a cop at his window and another poking around not far from Cutter's side.

"You headed to Fort Hasting? You'll need to head on around." The cop pointed, seeming about to give directions when Khalif stopped him.

"We're actually headed for 10, where it intersects with Long Pond Road."

"What, the Intercoastal United land?"

"Not the actual building. The land outside, where—"

"I know the place you mean. But …" His eyes narrowed, and he looked at Cutter. "Sir, if you don't mind, do you work at the hospital?"

"Yeah. I'm an orderly there."

"So you're registered?"

"What's that got to do with it?"

"Sorry, sir. I shouldn't have asked. If you'll just wait over there, sir, we should be ready to let people through presently." He pointed, then again looked at Cutter, and Cutter got the strangest feeling in the pit of his stomach.

The cop moved away, but Khalif called after him. "What's going on?"

"If you'll just wait a bit longer, sir." Then he was gone.

"What's that about, man?" Khalif steered to where others were parked, and a crowd — presumably the cars' occupants — stood idly, looking into the blocked-off land. "Why'd he ask if I had credentials?"

But that's not how Cutter saw it. The cop hadn't been looking for a *yes*. He'd been looking for a *no*. This was one of the very few times that the absence of an identity — not the presence of one — was required for entry ... or at least for information that was thus far being withheld.

They parked and got out. Khalif moved to the front of the barricade, shading his eyes and trying to see. Cutter circulated, trying to spot the crowd. He didn't know any of them, but a few wore looks of concern. Who were these people? But then a familiar face caught his eye.

"Dorothy!"

She saw Cutter and gushed, rushing toward him. Her big belly was now a blanket-wrapped bundle asleep in her hands.

They embraced as well as they could with a newborn between them.

Then the stories began. She reported no mysterious ten-thousand-ducat transactions from afar. She had relations, it turned out, near Phoenix. They'd taken care of her, paid her bills, and made sure she was well. Only now was Dorothy returning.

The others around them were all bound for the same basic area, far as she could tell. A lot were ghosts, denizens of an unregistered settlement fifteen miles or so from Amenity. Others were credentialed residents scattered through the area, temporarily denied entry. No one knew why.

"It just happened. What, maybe an hour ago?" She shrugged. "I almost got through, but then these cops came screaming out with their flashers up, and there was even a helicopter. *Two* helicopters. I'm with my folks."

Dorothy pointed to a pair of concerned-looking older folks drinking coffee served from the back of an ambulance with nothing better to do. "They figured they could just go right past, like when you see any cop with his flashers on, but then they turned sideways to block us like something from a movie. Then they're coming at the car with their hands up, saying like, 'Please sir, get back sir, it's no problem sir, but we just need you to hold tight.' Other cars came in behind us, but only the trucks got through."

Cutter had been watching Dorothy's parents, but his insides emptied with her words. "What?"

"All they let through were these automated trucks," she told him. "You know, like the ones on the news?"

Chapter Fourteen

LOOKING at Dorothy broke his heart.

Cutter had forced himself to become steely, pretending he was an outside observer and not someone intimate to this place. If he had kids, then right now, he'd be being strong for them. There were police to talk to. Investigators who pretended to care and news media covering the story from two sides so they'd be ready to play whichever one ended up being best: either a tragedy of hurricane proportions or a civic cleanup that was messy but had gone quite well. Either would work, depending on the audience.

"So you lived here, sir? *Lived?* Or *live.*"

The officer taking Cutter's statement was a twenty-something woman with painfully severe bangs. He found no sensitivities in her, despite his trying. Didn't mean she was a bad person, but she was probably numb. He had to remind himself that the official story here was still developing … and as of right now, the people of Amenity, though they were technically victims, were otherwise not coming off so well.

"Lived," Cutter said. "I've been gone for a little over half a year."

"Uh-huh. Uh-huh. And what was your business in returning?"

"I wanted to move back."

"Are you carrying any hazardous cargo, sir?"

"Hazardous? Like what?"

"Anything ATF might care about. Or the FBI."

"I don't know what you're talking about."

"Someone was supplying it, sir. These settlements, they're not patrolled for the most part. The kind of rabble that tends to hide domestic terrorists."

"Rabble."

"Apologies, sir. 'Census-denied community.' But it's true. A lot of bombers. Or napalm. They stockpile a lot of fertilizer. You can make ANFO from it."

"Napalm ..."

"Lots of it. Lots and lots and lots."

Cutter was going to ask about that when someone in an FBI slicker called the cop away. She excused herself, saying she'd be back when she obviously wouldn't. The three-letter acronyms were done here. He'd heard that there'd been explosives, but they'd been taken away and that there'd been a subversive cell, its members arrested.

Cutter and Dorothy and Khalif, independently, had all asked where the other residents of Amenity had gone because they sure weren't here, but the answers were an unhelpful, ironic restatement of what Boots always said about Cutter's father: *Couldn't say*.

Dorothy approached. She wasn't holding her baby. He assumed one of her parents had it. "Someone called in a tip. Said they were making bombs here."

"I heard." Cutter was trying to stay numb, to let none of this sink in. The sight of Amenity, obliterated, was too much to take. If he let the fear and horror and sorrow in, he wouldn't be able to think — and he needed that more than anything. "Nobody has any idea where they went?"

"Just Laurie and Kamal. You know Laurie and Kamal?"

He nodded.

"I think it's them. Based on the description and where they're saying they think the 'bomb factory' was. Laurie and Kamal were arrested. I think everyone else just ran. They think they were planning to blow something up, Cutter! Laurie and Kamal! Can you believe it?"

No. He couldn't believe it at all. The timing was all wrong, for one thing. It'd now been around ninety minutes since the blockade went up, and presumably, the blockade was raised because of the raid.

But the blockade also sounded like an emergency thing, whereas raids were usually planned ahead and coordinated between agencies. Someone he'd spoken to had been through Amenity on his way out, and the settlement had been whole and untouched around two and a half hours ago.

That left one hour in the middle after things being fine and the blockade going up. Dorothy had seen trucks enter, and someone else had seen trucks leave, and yet the FBI and ATF, so far as they'd tell Cutter — which wasn't much — said there'd been stashes of explosives taken away on those trucks.

So why had they entered so late … after the tip if there'd indeed been a tip? The whole thing reeked.

Cutter had also called Khalif in that missing hour. He'd asked for help, and all hell broke loose.

He took a few steps, trying to see the place for what it was. Agents had tossed most of the containers, but the violations weren't immediately visible. With the exception of a large hole that had been dug near Laurie and Kamal's place (maybe for all that supposed napalm and ANFO), Amenity seemed almost unchanged.

But it was shut down. The same, but stained. The feds would keep an eye on Amenity now. The whole point of places like this was to live off-grid — to be ghosts on purpose rather than poor folks who wanted credentials but couldn't get them.

Amenity had always been proud, like Boots and Cutter. But they wouldn't be able to live away from the census after this. They'd be checked-in-on, papers served — a scapegoat community for anything in the area that went wrong.

His childhood had died today, along with Dorothy's and that of everyone else. Every friend he'd had, every distant relative … and all of the belongings that Cutter always planned to claim upon his return, now in some federal locker forever.

"Cutter?" she asked.

But he'd gone from worried to afraid. From afraid to crushed. From crushed to despondent. And finally, from despondent to white-hot rage.

His fists had been clenched for long minutes, finger-nails cutting half-moons into the meat of his palms. The strength of his anger, when he finally saw it, came down like a hammer blow of revelation.

He hadn't seen it sneaking up on him. He wanted to hurt someone. He wanted to take what was left of Amenity's belongings to the agents who'd believe an anonymous tip over the word of several hundred honest, always-law-abiding but neglected citizens and shove it down their throats.

Furious. He couldn't hear or see correctly. Couldn't think. Could barely breathe.

"Do your parents have one of those wireless phones?"

"You mean a cell phone?"

He nodded.

"Yeah. They do. They didn't register me on purpose, you know. Hippies, in a way. They were planning to sell their house now that Dad's retired, come and live in … in Amenity with me."

There'd been the smallest hitch after *in*. Cutter wanted to take whatever had caused that errant emotion by its neck, then rip it to pieces.

"I need to use it. The phone. I need one of them to unlock it and authorize it for me. Now, Dorothy and I can't answer questions. Can you do that for me? Can you convince them?"

His tone was convincing. Dorothy nodded, then retrieved her father. He did as he was asked with a knowing, conspiratorial nod.

Cutter stepped away once the connection was made. The phone rang. Without being able to use a touchscreen, this was the only number he knew by heart.

Gord came on the line. He yelled at Cutter until Cutter calmed him down, explaining who he was.

"Oh. Cutter. Shit. I'm sorry. I thought it was them."

"Who?"

"I don't know. Someone who doesn't like you very much. Someone who wants to make sure I know *I* shouldn't like you very much. It's the same as before when the phone was ringing. I tried to do the Caller ID thing and to call the phone company back, but—"

"I know." He'd noticed the same when he'd talked to Jaxon-with-an-X.

"A bunch of guys came a few hours back. With guns. And someone sent me a picture of your car. *My* car. It—"

"I'm sorry, Gord. I'll make it up to you."

"Oh, fuck that! I told them I won't be intimidated. I shot at the people who came right through the fence. Dared them to return with a warrant. But nobody's come back. The phone just rings and rings. The one time I answered, some guy asked if you'd made it back to Amenity yet. Said you needed to learn to keep your mouth shut and that maybe I should, too. He said they can tell when we ping the GPS. And that they can track us wherever we—"

The phone was vibrating in his hand. Cutter looked at the screen to see another incoming call.

"Look, Gord. I have to go. Forget about me. I'm sorry I got you into this, and I'll pay for your car when I can. Do as they say and—"

Gord's voice became the panicked squeal of a deflating balloon. "Fuck that! Fuck all of that! I'm in this now, and someone needs to know better than to fuck with Gordon Frank!"

The second call rang again, from an unlisted number. Cutter thought fast; he no longer trusted phones. He no longer trusted anything that wasn't dirt and stone, wrench and steel.

"Listen really close, Gord. Go to where your favorite client lives. I'll meet you there in as long as you say your fat cousin takes his naps. You got me?"

Gord said very slowly and seriously, "Yeah, Cutter. I got you. I read you loud and clear."

"You can't drive your old car. Drive something else. Something unexpected. And bring toys. Lots and lots of toys, so all the children can play."

"Okay, Cutter. I'll do just that."

Taking the hint, Gord hung up. The second call rang a third time. Cutter answered but didn't say hello. He just waited.

Finally, someone — a woman this time, and not Marie — said, "So what do you think, Mr. Dunn? Do we understand each other?"

"You did this." He didn't say what *this* was or who he meant by *you*. Those things, he felt sure, were abundantly clear.

"Your friends were up to something," said the woman. "It's okay. They're not up to it anymore."

"I was going to let it go."

"But you didn't, did you? I could play it back if you'd like." Her tone became almost mocking. "'The man from Amenity, eager to dig up dirt and make an anonymous tip.' You were *let go*, Mr. Dunn. That's all. Those are the breaks. You were so worried about your girlfriend standing beside you right now that you lost your sense of right and wrong. You were no longer needed, so you were cast aside. You should be happy you had a purpose for a little while. That's really all that happened today: the cleaning up of a lot of people who had no real purpose. They were just … rodents. Rats. Roaches. Maybe they did wrong, or maybe they just *were* wrong. I don't really think it matters. They'll find new hidey holes. Roaches always do. As your grandfather was so fond of saying, 'the people of Amenity are survivors.' And they will. Survive. You'll let them do that much at least, won't you, Mr. Dunn?"

"Don't you touch them," Cutter snarled.

Dorothy was watching him from a distance. He saw the way her eyes widened as she watched his expression.

"You really just have to ask yourself a question, Mr. Dunn. All that happened, from end to end for you, was a return to your place. You came from nothing, and now you're back where you started. Your people were nothing and still are. Crawl back into your hole, little ghostie. You lost. Accept it, and we're finished."

SEAN PLATT & JOHNNY B. TRUANT

"Why should I believe you? How can I be sure that if I leave it alone, you won't bother us anymore?"

She laughed. "Oh, Mr. Dunn. It's adorable how much you think you concern us. How much you think you actually matter."

The call ended. Cutter let the phone sag, then looked out across his destroyed and scattered home: Boots Dunn, erased forever.

You play straight with the world, and it'll play straight with you. I'm makin' you a promise, you get me?

Cutter closed his eyes. It was a promise Boots shouldn't have made. One the world couldn't keep.

You stand up for yourself the way people here have their pride, and sooner or later, you gonna shine.

He opened his eyes. That second promise Boots made? That one, Cutter felt all the way down to his bones.

Dorothy went to take the phone from his hand and ended up taking his whole hand instead. She looked from him to Khalif. The small, thick man looked more furious than Cutter had ever, ever seen him.

"What are we going to do now, Cutter?" she asked.

He looked again at Khalif, then at her, and said one word:

"Shine."

Chapter Fifteen

DOROTHY AND KHALIF both insisted on coming along. Cutter wasn't surprised and let it happen over the protests of his internal Boots. He saw Khalif as an outsider and Dorothy as a woman, and in Boots' time, women were to be protected from the world's ugliness. Dorothy said goodbye to her baby — her coming along was as much about a future for that baby as it was about whatever might happen to Amenity and him.

But times had changed. Today's women of Amenity were harder than the men. Fiercer too. The few times there'd been thefts in Amenity from the outside, it was the women who'd led the charge to reclaim what was theirs. Dorothy had already seen ugliness; after Cutter told his story to her, she saw it in vibrant colors.

For Khalif, Amenity was more his family than was the outside world; it's simply the way his soul had grown. The idea of excluding either of them, once they resolved to go, would have been both arrogant and stupid. The one thing it had that the disassociated, lonely world he had spent his last half-year in didn't have was true community. If his friends wanted to join him, then Cutter was happy — and grateful — for the company.

"We can't drive," Khalif said. "You know that."

But it was even more than not driving. Dorothy and Cutter had no identification to trip either sensors or screens, but Khalif was chipped and worked in a local hospital. Cutter solved the Khalif problem by giving him the smart glass hat so he'd be invisible at best or be read as someone else at least.

Phones were out; near as they could guess, most of the tricks that had been pulled so far relied on tracking phones, maybe even turning on the mics or cameras that all the modern wireless ones had built into them. Lastly, there was the problem Khalif had mentioned: the fact that every single vehicle out there was plainly visible to the GPS grid ... which, as established back at Gord's place, meant they were visible to Hollander Sitwell.

Walking was their only real choice. At night. With Khalif wearing the hat so passing drones wouldn't scan and track him. Gord would need a hat, too — or maybe just to stay away from anything that would read his ID, the way people abstained from credit cards while on the lam in an old-time movie.

That part might take care of itself. Gord was antisocial at the best of times, and if he'd made proper sense of Cutter's message, he'd now be antisocial far from connected devices of pretty much any kind.

Fortunately, Gord, if he'd read things right, would be headed south while they walked north. Cutter had told him a conveniently misleading joke. Gord's "favorite client" was himself because he openly admitted to Cutter that he skimmed his own books to avoid taxes: an ironically micro-scale version of the much larger crime committed by Hollander Sitwell.

And while Gord literally lived at his office, he also had a hunting cabin in the woods. It was about halfway between them, and that meant with luck, a single long night of walking, assuming none of them were bitten by snakes, should see their arrival.

On the last two bits of the code he'd given, Cutter could only hope. But when they arrived, he saw that Gord had gotten both parts exactly right. Instead of driving literally any other car, he'd brought the truck Cutter had rebuilt by hand — the truck with no parts younger than fifty years old. The truck that, unlike everything else out there, had no tracking or parts even capable of *being* tracked. The truck that was invisible to everything but line-of-actual-sight … and hence as invisible to the world as Cutter himself.

Gord clapped Cutter and the others, who he didn't even know, in a manly one-armed hug. His face was grim. Pissed. He'd never imagined the man so serious.

"It's just the 'toys' left, then," Cutter said. "Please tell me you brought some toys."

Gord nodded. "For all the girls and boys."

He led them to the ghost truck, to which he'd attached a trailer as rust-covered and hence incognito as the cab. He rolled up the back door and turned on the light to what looked like a scrapyard.

Cutter had no idea how Gord had loaded the thing and done so quickly, but it looked as if he'd somehow packed his entire junkyard inside.

"They burned it, Cutter. Burned my whole business to the ground."

It led to an all-day discussion, then an all-night when nobody could sleep. They made a campfire, far away from everything. *Why* they needed to know. Hollander Sitwell was a glass company. They made a lot of things, but their roots were, and had always been, in glass. The future was still heads-up displays, like the smart windshield now doing camouflage duty inside Khalif's hat, but there had to be more to it.

There wasn't usually this much harassment when an ex-employee became a problem. Cutter had been angry about how he and the other fired truckers were treated, even though they blamed him instead of putting that blame where it belonged. But Cutter had long ago been willing to let it go. He'd wanted his pay, and he'd wanted to make sure Dorothy got part of it, and in the process of trying to get those things, he'd poked the wrong sore place … or so it seemed. Said the wrong things. Gotten the company thinking this particular pill of theirs might be poison.

Now it seemed they wanted to put their point in very dark and indelible ink. Interestingly, if Hollander hadn't pushed so hard, this would all be over now. Instead of only just beginning for Cutter.

"Hollander's been poaching my guys for years. You were just the latest." Gord nodded, his head dipping into shadow as the firelight moved up his face to his hair, then back to orange brightness again. "After yesterday's bullshit, with your people and mine, I made inquiries with some old friends."

"On the phone?" Dorothy asked.

Cutter had told her the supernatural ability his last chat had displayed, seeming to know he had her parents' handset and where they'd been standing during the call. It'd put her on edge and made her tell both Mom and Dad, out of what she hoped was an absurd amount of caution, to head out of town and lay low for a while.

Gord shook his head. "I figured that one out faster than you folks. Cutter'll tell you. We started poking around their smog control boxes, the ones that're tied to the GPS shit, and that's when things got weird. Phone rang, and it was one of his buddies." Gord nodded to Cutter. "Rang and rang after that. Eventually, I put it off-hook. You can still do that with hardlines, you know."

He shrugged. "First thing I did after that was call my girl Lucy. You remember Lucy, Cutter? At the hub 'bout the same time as you. I guess it don't matter. She used to work for Verizon. So I told her a bit of what was going on. Just a tiny bit, mainly that someone was harassing me on the phone, but I didn't say who it was or why. Somehow I mentioned the GPS thing too, though sideways so she wouldn't know it was related. And Lucy says, 'Yeah, you'd be surprised how insecure things like that are. It's all satellites. If someone has keys to one, they probably got keys to the other.' I figured you'd call, Cutter. Knew I'd be in trouble if you said the wrong thing — by then, I already had those folks outside my gate. So I was ready when you started talkin' nonsense. Looking for a code. And yours was a good one."

"It just doesn't make sense," said Khalif. "They're just a glass company."

Gord shook his head as if Khalif was teeing him up to make the point he'd almost forgotten. "Oh, it makes perfect sense. That's what I was gettin' at. Hollander's poached me for years. Ever since they started making smart windshields, their trucks came through here, and then *they* came through here 'just to check it all out,' and it was just like when I suggested you run repairs here, Cutter, and they paid you more to go with them instead."

"Gord, I'm—"

He waved it away. "Forget it. Like I said, ain't mad at you. Never was. Point is they done it before. Folks who used to work here still lived around here after Hollander, so I'd run into 'em. And guys. The things I heard when I found two of 'em yesterday, bought 'em a beer and got to talkin' about old times. Any'a you ever heard of 'vertical integration'?"

Heads shook.

"Usually, people talk about it like supply chain. Say a company makes steel girders using steel from a supplier, so when the first company expands, the first thing they do is buy out the supplier. Or maybe they sell those girders to distributors wholesale, so maybe they integrate *down* this time, 'stead of *up*, and buy out the distributors. The idea's to control as much as you can, up and down your core business. *Vertical*, get it?"

"Yeah, but what's that got to do with—?"

"Hang on. I'm gettin' to that." Gord re-situated himself around the crackling fire, crossing his legs underneath him. "You think of the smart glass business, there's all sorts of ways you could consider integrating vertically. But my girl Veronica, who did my accounting and then moved to their accounting department, she said Hollander thought about buying the vanadium mine first. Now with the smart trucks using the smart windshields, it's like they killed two birds with one stone because trucks are a big part of their customer base, and now they'll own the trucks and get to buy from themselves, but also now they're a shipping company, which makes them my competition, too. And okay, those 'integrations' are the ones you'd expect. But then Veronica said they started asking a really big question: *What's even higher, to integrate, than the vanadium mine?*"

"The money," said Khalif.

Cutter wasn't as surprised as the others, but the speed with which Khalif answered shocked him plenty.

"That's exactly right," nodded Gord, who hadn't seen that coming.

"I used to trade ducats a lot back when cryptocurrency was new," said Khalif. "After Bitcoin, when the feds suddenly had a good excuse to justify their actions against an unregulated currency market, I gave it up because why bother. Before the federal reserve took over, though, there was a lot of talk in the crypto space about how exciting some of the smart glass deals were, for ducats specifically. Because where were most of the transactions made — on smartphones, right? Smartphones are the second biggest market for Hollander glass, and only second because phones are small and windshields are big."

"I think I remember that," said Gord.

Cutter and Dorothy were shaking their heads. With the exception of Dorothy's parents' phone, Cutter doubted either of them had even held a smartphone ... let alone knew about the business done around them.

"Yeah," said Khalif. "I know there was a lot of discussion about monopolies and conflicts of interest. By then, almost all the smartphone glass was manufactured by Hollander, and almost all of the ducat transactions were being made on those phones through that glass, and the whole point of smart glass is that it's *smart*. Information doesn't just pass through it like light through a window. The glass *sees and remembers* whatever's displayed. It sees and *recognizes* the user. Any credentialed user can walk past any advertising screen to know that much."

Cutter nodded, hating the truth of what his friend was saying.

Khalif continued. "You walk into a store, and everything recognizes you. The door recognizes you and opens. The register recognizes you, so you don't have to take anything out of your pockets. Every advertiser recognizes you. And that's what people worried about: national standardization of a currency that was known, end to end with all its confidential user information, by one company's glass. Think about it. After enough time passed and enough people spent ducats, Hollander's databases would know more about America's financial ins and outs than the government. It was a giant problem for a while, but then it didn't seem to be an issue at all. It's like everyone forgot. But the forums had theories. They said Hollander got in bed with the government. Ducats happened — and happened in the *way* they happened — with the company's cooperation and permission."

Gord was nodding along as well. "That's pretty much what Veronica thought, seeing things from the inside. She told me something else, too, though. Veronica said she wanted to leave her job. The whole place toxic. It's run like an industrialized sweatshop. The top execs are paid far, *far* too much — like *where's-all-their-money-coming-from* too much — and everyone else might as well have whips cracking behind them. She got the feeling they were up to something, same as you. Manipulating ducats, maybe, even though federal audits and all the code shit they got is supposed to make that impossible. Squeezing suppliers for sure. Skimming off the top, maybe with and maybe without fucking with the ducats themselves, like I said. But Veronica won't leave. Says she's too afraid."

"Why?" Dorothy asked.

"Nothing specific. Just a vibe she gets. Maybe nothing. *Probably* nothing, she said. But Ronnie ain't here right now, to see the 'nothin' *we're* sitting in."

Cutter was taking it in. He didn't like where this was going, but he hadn't liked it for a while — since before, he'd nearly been crushed to a cube.

Based on his last phone call, it sounded like Hollander

was finally willing to lay down their side of this. But they'd stopped a few moves too late and made things personal.

"There's something else she told me," Gord continued. "Something that made my skin crawl. Over the years, a company makes a few arrests, right? I'm sure Nabisco's had an employee go apeshit on the cookie line once or twice, or Amazon's had assholes climbing their campus fences. I guess they usually call the cops. Sometimes they got a security detail that tosses them into a holding cell for a bit, like what people say about Disney Jail. Veronica told me Hollander's got private guards, too, only they dress like agents from *The Matrix* because I guess they want people scared. She heard 'em called 'executives,' but not the same kind that work in the tall buildings downtown."

Gord swallowed and spoke in something closer to a whisper. "They work for an organization-inside-the-organization called Promenade, which I guess is part of Hollander but also sorta separate from the company, and folks in security talk like they're Big Brother. Which probably they are. I mean, it's Hollander. Biggest maker of smart glass there is. I wouldn't put it past 'em to have every window made of the shit. Every monitor. Every bathroom mirror, shit, I don't know. Probably a billion eyes around that place, and the best part is they don't even need humans to watch all those eyes. Computers can do it. That's half what smart glass is, anyway. AI. Like your trucks."

The campfire circle was quiet. Cutter digested all he'd been told, nudging pieces until it made sense.

In a way, it all made *perfect* sense. Hollander was half company, half mob. They sold product, surveilled their customers and employees using that product, then leveraged all that gathered information in a *coup de grâce* that tied directly to the national digital currency.

No wonder they'd come out swinging so hard … and no wonder Cutter, now that he knew some of what was actually happening, felt so unwilling to let it go.

"Why does that make your skin crawl?" Dorothy asked.

"Because Ronnie said that when they have a fence-jump or unruly incident at Hollander, they call the cops like anyone else. But that's not what happens if something bigger happens, like this one time a guy tried to jam the gearbox running the assembly line. He was apparently possessed by some crazy conspiracy theory that probably wasn't all that nuts. Ronnie had to run to this little annex for some papers the next day. She saw the guy there, even though it was two full days later. He was tied up, slumped like a sack of shit, surrounded by these zoots in all black. I guess that's what happens with the folks Hollander thinks are really a problem: they take them to the annex."

"And … beat them up?" Cutter asked.

"Who knows? They got the execs to intimidate folks. The annex got no smart glass in it at all because that's where they send all the papers they don't want people looking at. The place don't exist, and neither do the folks there. Ronnie couldn't tell me one person she knows was let out of the annex. Now, that don't necessarily mean anything. Probably they just let 'em go and tell 'em never to show their faces again. Maybe they beat 'em a little first. Maybe a lot. Threaten their families, who knows? There's no record to say one way or the other. She said people talk like they just kill them folks. I think that's a bit much, but you know how a good rumor spreads."

It seemed Gord's story was done, and everyone knew tales of the other three. An unspoken question danced in the flames, and it wasn't a coincidence that Gord's horror tale about Hollander's black-box annex was the last story told. It was a warning — a perfect example of the stakes in their decision.

They could still walk away, easily even. Gord had lost his building and livelihood. Cutter, Dorothy, and to some extent even Khalif had lost Amenity ... and maybe its people; who knew if any would ever see the others again?

But the voice on the phone had promised Cutter that they were even-steven now, and if nobody struck back, this would all be over, and he believed it. But believing did nothing to change a system that was so horribly broken.

If they tried to fight and failed, Hollander's black ops might erase another community. One or all of them might end up in that anonymous annex as someone that nobody would miss if they simply disappeared.

But for Cutter at least, who'd grown up in a place where insults never went unanswered and where grudges — especially involving outside parties — were a matter of life and death, lying back wasn't an option.

Fight ... and die trying.

In a way, achieving both would be the best possible blessing ... at least for the sons and daughters of Amenity.

Chapter Sixteen

CUTTER DUNN WAS A WANTED man by the time they re-entered the world.

Either the company didn't think it could count on the man to keep his mouth shut despite their threats, or they wanted to make things difficult for spite, but it only took walking to the first gas station to see the problem.

Cutter's face graced every screen, surface, and pop-up ad on every smart-glass phone seen over a shopper's shoulder.

The four of them weren't carrying phones. Gord and Khalif now both wore smart-glass-lined hats after smashing a few choice items inside Gord's truck full of goodies. The glass didn't transmit after the device it was attached to; that much Khalif verified using a scanner Cutter made by disemboweling a welding rig and a comm panel, then joining them in unholy matrimony.

Smash the glass, and it was just glass ... except for the EM-refractive capability that made it "smart" when it was live and acted like a digital prism. That's why the hats worked. Information, like light, entered glass cubes from an outside source, then was read by the holographic matrix and stored there as long as the photocells held out. As the cells discharged, that information was radiated like heat. It confused sensors as Cutter's hat had done to provide him an identity back at the greasy spoon diner ... and in Khalif and Gord's case, it obscured those identities by fogging the signal with interference.

But what made the broken, repurposed, and ultimately recharged smart glass fragments problematic also made it useful. All those prism edges couldn't rightly process air signals, but they did catch them. Khalif, thanks to his early interest in crypto, had some facility with decoding signals if they were simply messy instead of deliberately encrypted.

So soon enough, they developed a system: Enter an area with one of the hats, then come right back out. The hat's glass bits would pick up digital chatter like the clothes of a person who falls into a pool will soak up water. Khalif would then use an optical measurement rig from Gord's scrap heap — employed long ago for truck repairs but rebuilt by Cutter's skilled hand for new purposes — to descramble whatever the fragments had collected.

It was piecemeal data collection, arranged by luck and trial and error like assembling a thousand-piece puzzle without knowing what picture was on the box.

Dorothy entered the truck's cab and handed the hat back to Khalif, with his shielded laptop, in the back seat.

"Good," he said. "Good."

"Good, how?" Dorothy asked.

"Just good."

"But I still don't understand what you're looking for. I still don't understand why we're doing this."

"Yeah, yeah," said Khalif.

He was focused, not dismissive. Cutter had never seen the man in his element; the days Cutter knew him were

Amenity days, where laptops and signal triangulation weren't exactly common. But Cutter, for his part, understood at least enough of Khalif's mission to know they had to keep doing it.

He was sampling Hollander's network, trying to triangulate the broadcast. Most seemed to be repeating off of old cell towers. Some were coming from and going directly to satellites. He was seeking a sensible way in — not a weakness, exactly, but a place where HS had intentionally opened a door.

"Main facility," said Gord. "Obviously. That's where we should start — at their big and obvious headquarters."

But the more samples Khalif collected from an ever-widening area, the more confident he became that the center of Hollander's signal collection — the covert stuff, meaning the signals it legally wasn't supposed to be collecting — wasn't at headquarters at all.

The goal was to cast a broad net, then triangulate. The source and repository of the illegal data collection (harvesting user data from pretty much every use whether they wanted it or not) wasn't likely to be interesting in and of itself, but Khalif was banking on HS having consolidated its wrongdoing.

If they were collecting illegal signals in one location, that same location was probably where Hollander kept everything it didn't want the world to know or see. They couldn't ping the GPS network again without raising flags, but the center of that particular effort was likely in the same place.

If Hollander was manipulating digital currency, it would need falsified documentation (that "double set of books" the loan man had suggested when Cutter first went to access his money) to support it. That, too, would be in the same place. Khalif, feeling creative, had started to refer to the mystery location of all Hollander's secrets as their "axis of evil."

Problem was, the so-called axis was hidden. Not at HQ as Gord suggested; that would be too obvious. They'd traveled to three states, visiting other large Hollander facilities and eliminating those locations as well.

They stopped wherever they could (wherever Khalif, reading digital signs that nobody else understood, told them to stop) and sampled whatever the signals gave them. They took turns with the hat, avoiding only Cutter. It went to Khalif, who entered the information into his laptop, then he'd pull up a map and tell them to go somewhere else. It'd been days. Cutter was getting anxious but knew there was really no other way.

If they were going to hurt Hollander Sitwell for what it'd done to Amenity and the rest, there was really only one logical location to punch: *the axis itself.* There'd be an antenna there, or a big old computer database, or something else Cutter couldn't fathom. So he trusted Khalif. His friend would find the building, and then they'd … attack it somehow. That part was unwritten. It was hard to form a plot when you didn't know where, when, or how to strike.

Dorothy handed the hat to Khalif at a truck stop outside Albuquerque. She fluffed her hair and said, "We need to head farther out. Gord is showing up on wanted screens now."

"The fuck?" Gord said.

But it made sense to Cutter. Dorothy was just one more citizen of Amenity; whoever-it-was had only called her father's cell phone because it was the one closest to Cutter. Khalif was a hospital orderly who'd taken a few days off, and nobody would miss. But the company knew that Cutter and Gord were buddies, and it knew they'd been plotting together at the Titan hub before burning it to the ground.

"Yeah," Dorothy said. "But it's random. I listened a little while I was in there. It's on the news, but there were also police inside. Shot in the dark, I assume; they can't know we're actually here."

"How do you know that?"

"Because it's a big mystery. You should hear the way they talk about you, Cutter." Her smile was incongruent — so much time away from her newborn was clearly raking her soul. "It's like what people would say about Batman. 'He's here, he's there, he's everywhere.' But I'm starting to think we really are invisible. They can't see it, or even imagine it, since nothing else out there has zero tracking chips, zero readable people riding inside. We're a hole in the world: a ghost truck with four ghost riders. It's like a superpower, I tell you."

This was not surprising. Really, it confirmed what Cutter was already thinking. There were more and more autonomous trucks on the road; the news reported that the company was 3-D printing and assembling ten a day. Those driverless trucks no longer traveled just between the vanadium mine and Hollander's Vegas fabrication plant; they were making client runs.

But most relevantly, the trucks performed perfectly so far as Cutter could see except for in one key way: *They never saw the ghost truck.*

Whoever drove needed to pass them quickly when they were en route from one place to another because if they passed slowly, those AI trucks would merge right into them. They'd drive up from behind, too, and fail to move aside when tailgated. For all intents and purposes, as far as the world's computers and GPS systems (and, more relevantly, Hollander Sitwell itself) had no idea their truck was even there. The thing was enormous, fully loaded, and completely invisible to anything but the naked eye.

There was one other thing. The truck and its passengers, although invisible to networks and systems and drones, was quite visible by conventional means. Perhaps even more visible than other trucks in that way because if anyone happened to note an empty parking lot on a screen and then see a truck right there in its middle anyway, red flags were instantly raised.

But, interestingly, most of those eyes belonged to truckers, either spying the ghost truck after failing to see it coming on their screens or seeing it parked at a gas station or diner. Those folks could have — and maybe should have — reported a truck with no ID, no responder, no virtual presence at all. But they didn't. Not once, as far as Cutter could tell. This despite catching familiar faces in trucker crowds more than once — faces that had been fired from Hollander's fleet, then rehired by competitors.

More than once, faces like that had spied Cutter — not just from the abundant *Wanted* footage, but more importantly from the day he was almost lynched on the Hollander grounds. Drivers who'd blamed him for the loss of their jobs. People who, on that day, had wanted him dead.

But today, something was different when they saw him. Something had changed. They saw the criminal, and they saw his old-school truck, and they saw how the vehicle didn't seem to exist outside of subjective experience. And to this, they did not react with alarm.

More than once, Cutter had seen someone see him and know what he was … and then nod in his direction, tugging the bill of a mesh-back ball cap like a modern-day gentleman doffing his top hat before a bow.

"They must be starting to figure it out," Dorothy said.

"They're stupid if they aren't. The news report I saw had added something about looking for suspicious vehicles. *Looking*. With your eyes. I hope you're about triangulated, Khalif. Eventually, the scare's going to wear off."

"Scare?" Cutter asked.

She smiled again. "Yeah. You know the superstitions about people like us? How we're blank, and if you're around us too long, we'll make you blank, too? You'll just sort of disappear? Someone's brought them all back. I've started to hear people talking in whispers, like they're afraid, like you really *are* Batman. Which I guess makes me Batgirl. As invisible as you are, Cutter, I'm even *less* visible. So what do you think? Time for me to try sneaking into the boys' locker room?"

Khalif finally looked up. "Just in time, then. I think I know where all the signals are originating." His laptop screen showed a satellite image overlaid with a stylized map. He pointed. "Here."

"You sure?"

"Pretty sure. Want the bad news? I'm sure mostly because of how hard it's going to be to get past all these fences, all these guards. It sure *looks* important if they're defending it so well."

Gord indicated a smaller, less interesting structure just away from the main building. "What's that?"

"It's exactly what you'd expect for HQ number two." Khalif punched in closer on the image, showing an unimpressive building with a simple shingle roof. "No signal coming from it. I'd guess it's because there's no smart glass."

Cutter's heart ticked faster.

"I think it's another annex," nodded Khalif, "where troublemakers go to disappear."

Chapter Seventeen

THEY STOOD over a huge sheet of drawn-on paper that probably wasn't entirely necessary. Khalif had sketched the plan and made it large because he seemed to think that's what you did when you planned something like this: you mapped it on a big piece of paper, which you unrolled dramatically and then stood around with other folks — ideally at some sort of arch-villain's war table.

"I guess first we should decide the goal," said Cutter. "It's inelegant, but I sort of figured we were just going to blow it up."

"No, no, no," said Khalif. "We go in at night. Get to the roof. Rappel down in catsuits."

"That's ridiculous," said Gord.

"Find the control room," Khalif continued. "Then we blow it up. Strategically. From the inside."

"Okay," Cutter said. "How."

It wasn't a question because Khalif's plan was more Hollywood than sensible. There was no answer, and Cutter knew it.

"What do you mean, *how*?"

"Well, do you still want to blow it up? Because I was mostly joking."

"Sure, man. Blow it up. How else do you destroy things?"

Dorothy moved in. "There must be a more elegant solution."

"To what?" Gord asked.

Cutter nodded. "That's exactly right. Solution *to what*? We don't have any idea what we're trying to solve. First the goal, then the way to do it."

"They're manipulating the foundation of democracy, man. The bedrock of everything. What else is there, other than blowing it up?"

"I don't see how that solves anything," said Dorothy.

"The first thing they'll say is that we're just terrorists. Like they said, Amenity was full of terrorists. You guys heard them. *Napalm. ANFO.*"

Khalif snapped his fingers. "That's it. ANFO. We ANFO the shit out of it."

"Okay," Cutter said. "What's your experience with ANFO?"

Khalif didn't reply.

"And it's small, too, right? Light. The sort of thing you put in your back pocket when you're spelunking down and balancing over the laser security grid. It comes in *bags*, Khalif. Huge bags, like forty-fifty pounds apiece. You have to haul in a shitload of them, then pack them with sandbags. Are they just going to make way, let us do all that?"

"You got a better idea?"

Cutter was thinking. He had the spawn of several ideas, but none were quite gelling yet. Misdirection would be most important. They were outmanned and outgunned, so the only option was to try and outsmart the enemy. If they went in hot, they'd be stopped at the door. No, if they really wanted to hit Hollander where it mattered, they had to do it like a magician pulling a trick. They'd have to flourish one hand, then attack covertly on the other.

"Come on, guys," Khalif continued. "They're all computerized, and none of us are hackers. We can't do anything elegant. One way or another, we need a bomb. We bomb it, and that opens an investigation."

"They'll cover it up," Dorothy argued.

"Then maybe we steal the computers instead. Bring them out here and see if others can hack in."

Cutter was shaking his head. "They'll just change it. Pretend we manufactured whatever we find."

"Our word against theirs? Okay, it's not perfect, but they won't have proof either. With the right coverage—"

"They'll *make* proof," Gord said. "That's what I'd do. If someone stole my shit, I'd pull the backups from the cloud and change it. Claim *they* were the ones who did it."

"Well, then, shit," said Khalif. "Are we giving up? Is that what you guys are saying … that after riding all over the place, after hiding out and apparently becoming Batman … we're just going to call it a day?"

"Nobody said we're giving up." Cutter was thinking of Amenity — how it'd been cleaned out completely over the past few days, shipping containers hauled away, and all those homes hollowed out. Neither Cutter nor Dorothy had heard a word about Amenity's citizens, nor even of the two people in federal custody, who should have been a matter of public record.

It smelled dirty. Filthy, even. Hollander's actions were unforgivable, and at this point, Cutter saw little reason not to play for keeps.

"What, then?"

"We need more information," Cutter said. "We need recon. We need someone to go inside, and look around, and tell us what's possible — the best way to hit them, so it's worth doing."

"Okay," said Dorothy. "Nobody knows me. I can just—"

"No." Cutter shook his head. "It has to be me."

"Why?" Khalif asked.

They weren't ready yet; Cutter had machinations in mind before even this part began. "Trust me."

AS CUTTER DUNN walked through the doors of Hollander Sitwell's supposedly unimportant but nevertheless extraordinarily well-guarded rural campus, he had a device inside his backpack that he'd built from electronic scrap from Gord's mobile junkyard. A sort of next-level sonar, able to image an area through walls.

It was old technology for ghosts, who'd never been able to tap into the virtual inventory used by connected citizens and therefore needed to improvise. Irrelevant technology for the credentialed world, which had no use for such things, but clever in the land of ghosts.

They needed a source and two receivers. The source was on Cutter. The first receiver was off-campus, held by Khalif. The third was the tricky one. It had to be between the two, off the perpendicular, somewhere near the loading bay. That same morning a frequent HS supplier called GingerGen had been robbed. Bombed with a small amount of ANFO, improvised from nitrogen fertilizer. Curiously, nothing was stolen despite clear intent to burgle. It was a non-event. The trucks meant for HS departed on time, and nobody noticed that one had new cargo ... including a small wave receiver in the back.

Gord hadn't liked that part: using an ordinary, trackable truck with a smart windshield as their delivery vehicle.

But Cutter insisted: a facility like this one wouldn't let just anything through its gates. The ghost truck, which Gord had wanted to use, would have set off all sorts of alarms.

The trick was misdirection. Whatever Hollander thought was happening, some deeper plan would have to lay buried inside it. Nothing unexpected could happen at the surface. They had to dissect what normally passed through campus, then make their plans, Trojan-style, inside them.

"Which is why it has to be me who goes inside," Cutter said. "I'm the most expected."

Not entirely true. Nobody, in a million years, expected the fugitive from the news to waltz through the doors of his nemesis's compound and announce his presence. But as far as Hollander was concerned, Cutter Dunn worked alone. His accomplices would need to hang back. They'd be there for round two when the plan roared forward from recon-naissance to action.

Getting in was easy. Getting out, after doing his recon, would be harder. But that's where the hijacked truck's cargo came in.

The doors opened. The doors closed. He'd passed the gate in a "borrowed" and hotwired car, wearing the glass hat. It had confused the gate sensors into thinking the guard he spoke to was in the car as well: two copies of the same man in the same place.

The guard wrote it off as a glitch, shrugging at Cutter's crudely forged ID because nobody used hard-copy identifi-cation anymore, which was exactly why Cutter made it. He told Cutter to present at the front desk. They'd decide whether the guy with the glitchy ID would be allowed in or not.

Of course, the security desk was a bit more advanced than the guard at the gate, seeing as it was the theoretical last line of defense before unwanted personnel went further into the sanctum. It saw through the glass hat the second Cutter made it through the door.

The lobby was large, electric-lit, with only the glass doors for natural light. Cameras and motion detectors were everywhere, uniformed watchmen visible beyond the desk, watching the halls and rooms beyond.

Guards approached, hands on weapons. Cutter was stopped halfway between the door and the desk.

"Who are you?" the first guard asked.

"Can't you just scan me?"

"Scanner's glitching. Let me see some ID."

"I'm sorry. I don't have any."

Then he lowered his hood.

The guards, having seen Cutter's face everywhere recently like the rest of the world, reacted immediately.

One stepped back. The other went for a walkie-talkie, muttering commands into the mouthpiece.

"Hands up!" said the first guard.

"You think I have a weapon?"

"I SAID HANDS UP!"

"I don't need one. Because I *am* a weapon." Cutter raised his hands overhead. Taut steel drawstrings that ran from each wrist to his waist pulled tight, flipping a switch.

Inside Cutter's backpack was a heavy array of over two thousand mostly depleted batteries scavenged from Gord's truck full of garbage. The residual charge, when triggered by the drawstrings and the switch, was plenty to trip the automobile ignition coil also in the pack.

The coil shot a few thousand volts through Cutter's improvised electromagnetic pulse bomb. The lights went out as Cutter hit the deck, and by then, people were already screaming. Everyone knew by now that ghosts had been sandbagging society. They'd always been able to disappear — and to make those who came too close disappear as well.

Cutter wasted no time. With the lights out — a surprise he'd known was coming because he'd raised his hands to flip the switch — he had a few seconds advantage. He sprinted hard toward the northern corridor, body-checking the first guard to come at him.

From here, he had to guess. They knew only the rough geography of the building, but the loading docks were north.

He took the first right, hopefully into the dock itself, and found the door still locked. Apparently, when the power died, they locked everyone inside.

Cutter pulled the pack from his back, the guards already recovering and just seconds away. He yanked the coil leads from the EMP, stuck them against the lock's plate, and triggered the switch again.

Power arced through the leads; there was a spark and a sizzle; the door clicked like a mechanical hiccup but did not open.

Cutter glanced back and, seeing the guards fumble forward in the darkness, did the only thing he could think to do — reared up and kicked the door just to the right of the lock.

The tripped thing was only stuck and swung violently inward.

Cutter followed it, shoved the door closed, then emptied his pack for the final item hiding inside: three simple, small wooden wedges.

He used his shoe to hammer them into the gap between the door and the frame.

A shout. Then a bullet smashed through a small rectangle of glass at eye level. A hand came through next, but there was no harm in it; the handle and lock were nowhere near, and anyway, the wedges were the real problem for them now.

Still, Cutter jammed the coil leads into the hand, causing a jaw-clenching, spasming sound to bleat from the other side. Then he removed the coil and batteries from the pack and set them at the door's foot, tossing the mostly empty pack back onto his back.

This done, he used duct tape to fasten the wire from the coil to the door, so the two bare leads poked up where the window had been. Anyone else who decided to reach in would now get the same electric surprise.

He moved away from the door, looking around in the darkness and realizing he'd made a mistake; he wasn't in the loading dock after all. An abortion of a device was tucked into his belt: a plain old citizen's band radio made from a coded two-way's guts plus crystals and a lot of coiled copper wire. An organization as advanced as Hollander Sitwell didn't think to search for — let alone block — anything as low-tech as a child's CB.

"Outside Outside. Do you read me?" he said into the thing.

Khalif's voice came back. "I read you, Inside."

"Bit of a hitch. Ended up in the wrong twenty. I need some alternatives. Advise."

"Inside," said Dorothy, who wasn't supposed to be involved with this part. "I have an idea."

"Who are you?"

"I'm Inside Two. Stand by."

"Stand by for what?" This was all already out of control. Cutter had been ridiculous to think it was possible. He'd gotten in, okay, and he'd shut off the lights and gotten past the guards, also okay. He'd gotten into a room, just as planned and barred the door. But they'd been counting on a bit of luck: Cutter managing to actually enter the loading dock based only on assumed geography — down the north hall, the last door on the right should have been the dock. He'd stopped one door too early. Apparently, there was one more door, and he'd neglected to see it.

Sixty seconds in, and it was already over. He was trapped in the wrong place, without the gear he'd been counting on, and there were guards outside who'd make their way in eventually, either before or after they got the power back on.

He had no weapons, no way to fight back or fight his way out. He'd been counting on the damn truck. The whole thing was supposed to be an insane berserker run, rationalized as genius without any better ideas.

Cutter would pull away and make it to cover, then they'd have a facility map (thanks to the sonar he carried) and could maybe make a plan for real. But now it was all clearly stupid, and clusterfucks abounded.

Dorothy wasn't even supposed to be here.

"Come back, Inside Two. Say again. Stand by for *what*?"

There was nothing. A great clanging was now coming from the next room: guards, surely, massing and calling for backup.

A tremendous noise, like ships colliding, came from everywhere around him. The wall shook, and plaster sifted. There was a loud, rhythmic beeping and a whir of gears or wheels, then the same collision sound repeated.

Something massive PLOWED through the wall. It was yellow, and had giant prongs on the end, and was being driven by Dorothy.

"Where the hell did you come from?"

"Loading bay, idiot." She grabbed his sleeve and pulled

171

past the forklift she'd driven through the wall and into the next chamber.

"Where the fuck were you?"

"In the truck." Dorothy pointed. The rear was pulled up, and to one side, Cutter could see the blinking receiver of his sonar array.

"Who let you in the truck?"

"Me."

"Who else?"

"*Me*, Cutter. Are you going to keep standing there like a dipshit, or are you going to help me unload?"

Cutter couldn't think straight. It felt like a mutiny. The plan was always for him to blow the facility's power and then haul ass through it to the waiting truck. *Alone.* He wouldn't be able to drive it, but he could jump through the door and then through the fence, which theoretically Gord was supposed to clip an escape hole into.

They weren't planning to hit the facility now, just to scope it with sonar. Yet here was Dorothy … and he couldn't even argue because she'd just saved his ass. Maybe he wasn't alone in the world after all.

"Unload what?" Then he had it. "No. Oh, no. You guys went with Khalif's plan."

"Only halfway." Dorothy was dragging him to the open rear. "We didn't have much ANFO. Fresh out of napalm, too, of course."

"Of course. But …"

"Cheer up, Cutter," Dorothy said. "I'm not happy we were right, but we were right. You wouldn't have gone along if you'd known we had this part in the bag, but you're about to be really happy we did because your plan was shit, and this one is rather terrific."

"No." He was shaking his head. "This is too off the cuff. You have to plan for something like this."

"Spoken like a man. No wonder it's always us who go on the raids."

Now he led toward the gap between the backed-in truck and the open door. He was preparing to jump down when Dorothy grabbed him.

"No." She pointed at something he couldn't see until he did.

Just as she'd predicted, but he hadn't believed, the grounds were now swarming with guards. Cutter thought he could run for the fences? He'd vastly underestimated this facility's importance.

"Jesus. You undid it all."

"Not the finale. Just the middle. You were right, Cutter: *misdirection*. Show them one plan, but your real strategy is something else. Now help me. Keep your balls in your sack because you've still got the big switcharoo to play. So say it straight. I know this surprised you, but did it fuck you up? Tell me if it did, Cutter, and I'll do it if I have to."

Instead of answering that (things were happening too fast to think, let alone about the plans behind the plans), Cutter ran into the truck's rear. There wasn't supposed to be anything in here: just normal cargo meant for HS from GingerGen, plus their receiver.

But that's not what he saw as his eyes adjusted. He'd think they managed to swap one entire trailer for the other if he didn't know better. It looked as if Gord's entire scrapheap was still inside ... but so were all their tidy little inventions, meant for Round Two but stepping into the spotlight early.

They were all on casters. Cutter rolled them out. "What's this?"

"Glass," he said, shaking a box of it.

"Smart glass?"

"Regular glass. Untempered. And gloves. And glue."

"For what?"

"Like a porcupine. Use your imagination."

"I don't remember this part," Cutter told her.

"Yeah, well. I was in that truck for a long time."

"You were *inside the truck*?"

"Sensors can't see me any more than they can see you. Who else was it going to be?"

The door shook. Like in the previous room, it seemed Dorothy had entered the bay when Cutter unlocked the facility with his EMP, then crossed the loading dock to jam wedges into the doorframe. Walls between the hallway and rooms were cinder block, but in time they'd manage to smash through the door themselves.

Cutter was shaking his head.

She grabbed him and slapped his face. "You knew this was always the plan. Khalif told you trying to recon first was a bad idea, and I'd like to see you argue now that it wasn't. We set things up for Stage Two right away, was all, because nobody but your dumb ass thought the company would just sit back after you ran through here with sonar and let us try again. So it's still the same plan. This is Day Two, is all. Now. Last time. Are you with me?"

"I'm with you."

They rolled out the devices. All made of scrap, just like Amenity's good old days. Cutter touched an auger blade, sharpened.

"There's something else you should know," Dorothy said.

"What?"

"Laurie and Kamal."

"Laurie and Kamal?"

"They tried to break out of custody today. You know, because they're terrorists. They were shot and killed. Gord overheard it. You think Laurie masterminded a prison break?"

Laurie was seventy and out of shape even then. The idea that she and her husband had escaped was as ridiculous as the notion that they were terrorists in the first place.

Cutter's moment of confusion was almost gone. Dorothy's words banished it the rest of the way. His hand tightened on the sharpened auger. Blood trickled down one palm.

"Yeah," she said. "Me either."

"Okay," Cutter replied. "Let's go."

THE GOAL now was to make as big a showing as possible, then find a way to reach the mainframe for the big light display before their escape. Cutter wished the truck could be driven, but of course, it couldn't be unless one of them could somehow ID as its proper driver. He wished it was his own ghost truck, but of course, that vehicle was spoken for.

They could no longer run for the fences; they couldn't hide inside the trailer because the guards would look there as soon as they entered. There was nowhere in the building to run that wasn't somehow covered.

They were in trouble. Big trouble. Cutter was already writing off the "and escape" part of the mandate. There was a lot more security than anticipated — something Cutter might complain was a reason they should have gone with his recon-only plan if that reasoning wasn't so obviously flawed; recon-only would have failed even worse.

He and Dorothy might die here — or, more likely, they'd be captured and tortured. Hollander would torture Cutter to find out what he knew and who he might have told.

He keyed his radio, hoping the guards banging on the doors wouldn't hear his half of the conversation. "Outside, Outside. Did you see the mainframe from my sonar?"

"Still trying to find it," came Khalif's voice.

"Maybe we don't need the mainframe," Dorothy said to Cutter.

"We need the mainframe."

"We can't reach it even if they find it. We don't need the mainframe, Cutter. We can find a way without it."

"Listen to me, Dorothy. *We need to reach the mainframe.* This falls apart without it. We—"

A boom shook the loading bay door.

"Load," Dorothy said.

They prepared the devices. Loaded the weapons. Set them up. They were both looking around, trying to see a way out of the room, when the radio crackled: "Inside One and Two. I think we have our target."

"Where?" Cutter asked.

"Three rooms south. You ran right past it."

Cutter swore under his breath, but it's not like he could have known that.

"It's okay." Dorothy pointed. "The forklift."

But she'd broken it irreparably. Something in its guts just whirred and whirred — a gear missing its mate, maybe, and something Cutter could surely fix if he had time … which he did not.

The door buckled, then burst open behind them. A tripwire triggered the three tamping guns they'd rigged to fire Gord's vast stockpile of rusty drill bits, and they went off brilliantly. A spray of blood decorated the back wall as bodies fell. Cutter thought he saw a head roll away.

Guards spilled through the gap. Cutter looked up, saw a ladder along a high-up catwalk, leading through a skylight far above the floor.

"The roof. GO!"

Dorothy went. Cutter stood back, reloading the guns. The guards swept past him, knocking him down, but then passed him by for Dorothy.

Cutter gave chase, taking one by the ankles. He pulled a large actuator lever on one of the other defensive machines they'd made: a repurposed rock drill with a three-foot-wide auger on the front in a sadistic corkscrew.

The lever lowered the auger. Cutter kicked the guard into place, then pulled hard on the lever. Now only the pressure of the auger in the man's chest was holding him in place. "I don't want to hurt you."

The guard could still reach his holster. His gun was out in a flash. He took aim at Dorothy, who'd almost made it to the first of several ladders, this one leading up to the catwalk.

"NO!"

He fired. Dorothy fell into a motionless heap.

Cutter looked the guard in the eye.

The gun came toward him.

So Cutter hit the switch, rolling the counterweights. The thing didn't require electricity. It cut a hole through the man large enough that it was almost comical, only small thin strips of meat connecting the top half of his body to the bottom.

The guard screamed before dying, and Cutter yelled for them to come at him and leave her alone.

The guards instead ran faster up the ladder to where Dorothy still seemed to be moving, trying to turn over.

Truncheons out. They began to beat her.

Cutter reached for a hammer. A wrench.

Saw red.

And became the devil.

Chapter Eighteen

BEFORE CLIMBING THE LADDER, Cutter stepped into an industrial sprayer that Hollander Sitwell used for the assembly of adhered parts and the application of certain ionic paints. It was filled with something far more viscous than paint today. This complete, he revisited Dorothy's invention, which was on the floor beside the dead man with his missing core.

Thirty seconds later, he was running across the loading bay floor with an improvised crossbow in one hand, a rebuilt skeet-thrower in the other, and a plumber's wrench and ball-peen hammer tucked into the back of his belt.

It was amazing what you could build with your hands if you were outside the box as Boots said Cutter had always been — not inside it like those who only thought digital.

Cutter could barely see. He was too furious, all that restrained anger finally bubbling up to the surface. Seeing them swarm, Dorothy had done it. They went at her with truncheons like 1930s beat cops, not bullets and lethality.

They'd pay for it.

Just like they'd pay for Amenity. Like they'd pay for Boots, who'd died peacefully but had never risen in the world he loved rambling through so much just because he'd been born without papers and never been given a chance to gain them.

They'd pay for Laurie. For Kamal.

They'd pay for the society they built and the lies they told and the money they minted for themselves to wallow in, sharing only when they had to.

They'd pay for cheating the system that lessers could never cheat. For rigging the game.

They'd pay for who they were, what they wished to become, and the ways they'd gone about it.

Cutter gave himself to them, just as the others gave themselves. And now they were trash? Now they were just colonies of roaches — an infestation to be cleansed from the streets?

The crossbow fired a three-headed bolt made from the heavy body of hedge-clippers. They'd welded only one round because they'd had only a single spring small enough but strong enough to close the shears. The edges were razor-sharp, literally.

Cutter had exactly one shot but made it perfectly, spearing one of the guards beating Dorothy in the shoulder, causing him to screech, and when the shears clamped shut, and his arm flew off, he screamed even louder.

Cutter stood back, secured the clay-pigeon thrower onto a bench-mounted vise, and crouched behind to aim it. These rounds he had three of: each a petri dish with its halves secured with Scotch tape, full the guts of miniature clockwork toys. The ends of the clockwork were equipped with barbed talons, so they'd embed themselves in skin or clothing and stay there, plus triangle-shaped sections of razor blades attached to the armatures. They'd tested one on a bucket of fried chicken. After deployment, the meat was untidily sliced for consumption, no longer on the bone.

Three petri dishes to a hopper.

Belt fed, one at a time.

Voice-activated. All you needed was the password.

The guard between Cutter and the man he'd de-armed had turned and was descending, going for his gun, either disobeying the boss's orders and prepared to kill or hoping he had good enough aim to merely wound.

Cutter marched forward with insane bravado, half-hoping the guard would end him. The gun was up, but then light must have flashed from the skylight because Cutter saw reflections streak his face.

His arms went up. His face squeezed in confusion. Cutter stepped around the gun, used the wrench to break his wrist, then used the ball end of the hammer to turn his skull to paste.

With that, the two remaining guards began to descend.

"PULL!" Cutter cried.

The guards stopped, wary, then continued when nothing happened.

And then something happened. The trigger pulled the first petri dish full of clockwork scavengers into the throwing arm of the pigeon-hurler, then let it fly.

The dish hit the man, broke open, and covered him with tiny whirring robots. At first, there was nothing, but then they made their way through his skin and began to fillet him alive.

He lost his balance and fell to the ground, neck broken.

The last man came with an air of resignation as if stopping to deal with Cutter instead of beating the woman was a terrible inconvenience.

Cutter fired the last two petri dishes, but the man had

seen the threat coming and stayed back, kicking the tiny slashers away.

He grabbed Cutter by the jacket, meaning to throw him off or bring him in. But the glue Cutter had applied below was dry by now, even on his skin where he'd been unable to keep it away, and the box of broken glass *(Like a porcupine. Use your imagination.)* had stuck quite nicely to his clothes.

The guard grabbed.

Felt the skin of his palm slit to ribbons.

Cutter hit him hard across the jaw with the plumbing wrench. He spun lazily downward, landing in a large circle of new guards now waiting at the bottom.

They looked up. Shouted. Began to climb.

Cutter rushed toward Dorothy's inert form as bullets flew.

He advanced, flinched back, advanced again. Bullets pinged off metal between himself and Dorothy.

Go, said the practical voice of reason: Boots' voice. *You can't carry her out of here. Get to the mainframe. If she's dead, she's dead, and if she's alive, you can't help her yet anyway.*

He was up the ladder in seconds. There he found the roof blessedly flat and bathed in daylight. A second group of guards was coming out of the next-room skylight; it seemed every room along here had one. The sun struck Cutter and the sharp glass he'd covered himself in, lancing spots of sun back to dazzle them like chasing a mirrored disco ball.

He had no weapons left except his hammer and wrench. He ran south, headed for the third skylight down.

The guards gave chase. Cutter reached the window first, but it was latched. He pulled, tried to pry, and eventually drew his hammer to break it open.

He was over the hole when the shots came, zinging past his ears.

Someone yelled, "NO! THEY WANT HIM ALIVE!"

The shooting stopped.

Cutter put one foot in the hole, unable to quickly find which side held the ladder. He took too long; rough hands grabbed him and yanked back fast.

Blood spattered Cutter's cheek as he found the top rung, as he tried to shake off more grabbing hands, as, in his confusion, he lost his footing and slid down the ladder like laundry down a ribbed washboard.

The fall was short but painful. Cutter struck a raised, grated metal catwalk six feet below the skylight, his ankle twisting and something popping as it went.

He pogoed upright, high on adrenaline, ignoring the pain as a matter of life and death. The ceiling was low up here, though, and he struck it hard.

Legs descended beside him. Cutter wrapped his arm around them, then dropped down with all his weight to the catwalk, squeezing as he went.

Pants and skin became confetti. The man who owned them fell untidily atop Cutter, who ran before more could arrive.

He made it to the floor through shouts and the occasional gunshot, purposefully wide to alarm but not hit him. He could see the mainframe behind panels of glass in what struck him as a cleanroom. Inside were racks and racks of tidy rectangular computer elements, the backs of which were a banded forest of cables and wires.

"STOP! STOP WHERE YOU ARE!"

Cutter double-timed, thinking that *now* they might shoot; *now*, with the servers in danger, things might be too far gone to bring the prisoner in alive.

He had only one small bomb. Nitroglycerin, stabilized

through means only Gord claimed to understand, sweated painstakingly from old construction dynamite given covertly to Gord as a saboteur's present.

It wasn't a truck full of ANFO, and he had no sandbags with which to pack it. It couldn't possibly do enough, could it?

Put it in the middle. Squeeze it between all those racks, and maybe it'll do some damage.

Shots fired — *at* him this time.

Glass walls shattered; one fell to bits.

Cutter couldn't shove and run; all he managed was to squeeze his whole self into the space he'd meant only for the bomb.

He was surrounded. They came slowly, no longer in a hurry. There was nowhere for Cutter to go — and less with every passing second.

Soon he was in the dead center of all the servers, or the mainframe, or whatever the people here called such things. He held the bomb up, finger on the detonate button.

"I'll do it," Cutter said to the ring of aggressors. "Touch me, and I'll do it right here and kill us all."

But then something cold and metallic pressed into Cutter's neck from behind as fifty thousand volts pressed into his nervous system.

The taser loosened his grip. Loosened his bladder. He pissed himself as he slumped to semi-standing, unable in the confined space to truly fall.

The bomb hit the floor, harmless and undetonated.

Chapter Nineteen

THE EXECUTIVE — *Nicola* — waited until she was sure Cutter was finished with his story. Then her head bobbed.

"So there *was* someone else. You were lying to me."

Yes. He'd lied. He'd told her about Dorothy but not Khalif or Gord, both of whom had never entered the complex and were, he assumed, safely away.

Lying up front and then revealing Dorothy later was a way to make Nicola think he wasn't thinking straight. A taser to the neck was no joke, and Cutter was lucky, there were still cards to play.

"Is she alive?"

"I don't know, Mr. Dunn. Was she with you in the first place, or were you alone the way you first told me?"

"Obviously, you knew about her. I didn't think you needed me to feed you with a spoon."

"Hmm. Well. I'll tell you what I think. I think you're full of shit. I think you had other help, and you slipped, and maybe if I keep twisting, you'll do it again."

Cutter eyed the other person in the room. Barely a kid,

and he looked like an intimidated person trying hard not to flinch. His eyes went back to Nicola.

"When did you put the glass spike on your boot?" she asked.

"On the factory floor."

"When?"

"Before the door was kicked in."

"I see. Here's my response. You ready? *Bullshit*."

"When do *you* think I put it there?"

"Not bullshit about the glass. Bullshit about the whole thing. You walked right into our facility. Right to the front door. You couldn't possibly have been planning to blow the lights, then just hoped you'd make it to the computers on your own. You don't strike me as that stupid. So here's what I think: I think something went wrong. I think you improvised, then got caught with your pants down. I think the real plan was some sort of a coordinated assault. Seeing as we can no longer find *any* of the people who used to live in your settlement …"

Cutter sat up straighter. A sharp edge cracked, then poked him just a little. They'd left him in his glass-covered clothing, wrestling him into the off-grid annex with heavy gloves. Did it really matter if they were going to beat and kill him anyway? That kind of thing could be done without touching.

"The people of Amenity? You don't know where they are?"

"Don't play dumb with me, Mr. Dunn. Maybe they didn't have ANFO and napalm when we raided the place, but I'm willing to bet they can make it. That's the thing about you people. Rats can survive on anything. Make do with anything."

"They weren't involved," Cutter said. "I swear. I haven't even seen them."

She looked hard at him. "Then who, if not them?"

"Dorothy. Me and Dorothy."

"That's not enough people. Maybe you believe your own hype, but I sure don't. I have no idea how you eluded us for so long, showing up here and there without ever being in between, but you're not magic. You put on a little show up at main, blowing the power just by raising your hands, but I saw the rig. *Ghosts.*" She scoffed. "That nickname's a mistake. Makes people superstitious."

Nicola glanced at the kid, who was clearly a filing tech instead of a guard. *Jason.* Cutter had heard her call him Jason. He'd been keeping his distance, afraid to approach Cutter … and not just because he was covered in glass.

"Truth," she said.

"What time did you say it was?"

"Late enough that the sun's set. So what should I expect from you now? Lies?"

"You should expect *something.*"

"But not lies?"

"I'll make you a deal," Cutter said. "Truth for truth."

Nicola sat back.

"I mean it. I don't think I have much left to lose. You can't let me go, can you? So you won't."

She said nothing, maybe because the clerk was standing right there. This was supposed to be two executives — ideally, one of them being Jaxon-with-an-X — instead of an executive and a stand-in. That was Cutter's fault. He'd been angry about Dorothy; he shouldn't have kicked her partner in the balls.

"So there's no reason not to talk to me. Come on, Nicola. Let's do this man-to-woman."

She leaned in, unsure what to think of this strange man.

"I'll just say things, then. You can let me know if I'm right."

"Why does it matter?" Nicola asked.

"Because I was told by a great man that if I played straight with the world, it would play straight with me."

Her eyes went to Jason. She nodded, and he backed up. He almost kicked the backpack Cutter had been wearing as he went, now emptied of its contents after being taken from his back. He could see its insides, shining with silver like the innards of a pizza man's delivery bag.

Jason waited, but he wasn't far enough back. Nicola nodded again, and he took the hint. He moved all the way out the door and into the other room, soundproofed now from this sensitive conversation.

"Okay," she told him. "Go ahead."

"This was always about money," Cutter said.

"What else is anything about?"

"The company keeps double books. It shouldn't be possible, but somehow they're doing it. I'm guessing it must be, like I said, ducats started with Hollander Sitwell. Ducats and lobbyists — two for the price of one. They've rigged the minting, is that right?"

"Keep going."

"Far as I can tell, there's a correct ledger out there somewhere. On the public books. Most of the time, the paper records trotted out for the auditors come from the annex at your headquarters. Except when you need to prove something that isn't technically true."

Nicola almost smirked.

"Like when my buddy Jaxon-with-an-X needs to make a withdrawal on money he shouldn't technically have. Or like when you erase folks, the way you erased me."

"Now, how exactly would that work, Mr. Dunn?" she asked.

She wasn't saying *No*.

"The real records of money in and out of Hollander is what the federal auditors normally see. That's like baseline. You keep your real fraud separate — and that's stuff that 'corrects' the baseline. It's like the headpiece to the Staff of Ra."

"What?"

"In *Raiders of the Lost Ark*. There's this headpiece that tells you how long the stick it's mounted on is supposed to be, but it's a cocktease. One side says, 'Make the staff this long.' Then the backside says, 'Haha, fooled your ass! Take back a foot or so and make it shorter.' I figure your ducat records are like that. The real records say, 'Jaxon has this much. Cutter Dunn has this much.' Legit. But then records somewhere else change those numbers. They're the backside of the headpiece: 'Add this much bullshit to Jaxon's income. Subtract this much from Cutter's income.' *Corrections*, not full false records. It's the only way you could have stayed invisible for so long."

Her head bobbed slowly. "I figured all of you were stupid."

"All of whom?"

"Ghosts."

"For the longest time, I couldn't figure out where you kept the other records. The bogus ones. They'd be on paper. Just one copy, not backed up, because they're evidence. I really wanted to get at them. I just couldn't figure out how."

Nicola looked around at all the paper records Jason spent his days filing, then shrugged. "Kind of stupid after all, then."

"But smart enough to wear a second set of clothing," Cutter told her.

That didn't make sense. Her head cocked like a curious dog. "What?"

"You know," Cutter said, straining up now so that his glass-covered shirt caught on the table, pinning it down, letting the bright silver garment beneath to show at his neck. "It wasn't really making a self-driving truck that was so difficult. It was getting it to *stop* that was the problem."

Nicola bolted upright. A whine had been growing outside, now obvious as an approaching engine. She closed the distance to Cutter, then pinched a glass-free section of shirt between her fingers and ripped it open.

Beneath was his asbestos-lined fire suit, as useful in the coming moments as when he'd planned this.

She looked at him with horror. The engine increased its volume. Cutter found himself smiling in her face.

"If you don't care if it stops, the rest is easy. You just need some sort of a GPS beacon to tell it where to go … like the one I swallowed before I walked through the door."

The engine hit a fever pitch. No brakes; no need.

Nicola bolted from her chair and took one step toward the door, but she was far too late. The truck, invisible before it became the only visible thing in this corner of the world, hit the annex at a full barrel.

Cutter rocked his chair hard left and started to crawl, hoping the steering couldn't course-correct to follow him those final few feet as it smashed through the wall.

It didn't; the napalm inside the cab ignited the way Khalif had predicted, and the entire behemoth cut Nicola the executive nearly in half on its way to a hard stop against the opposite wall.

Heat came in a wave. A small burst bomb inside scattered the liquid fuel, but Cutter was low and protected at first by a cabinet. Some coated his legs, burning the outer layer of his clothing quickly away.

The fire suit was protecting him for now, but he'd have to be fast. He didn't know if napalm burned with much smoke, but the fraud papers in here sure would ... and even staying below the smoke, his head wasn't exactly fire-retardant enough to save him.

He had literal seconds before the fire was everywhere. It spread slower than a Vietnam airburst but still very fast. Cutter's hands were still bound; he wore no gloves so would have to roll and sit on them in hopes that protection was enough. The bigger issue was his hair, his face, his cranium.

He wiggled as fast as he could, shoving himself inside the emptied backpack, trying his best to roll no-handed so its flapping edges would snag on something and allow his body movements to pull the neck hole tight.

It was very quickly what felt like several thousand degrees. He had the disguised flame hood on and had gotten himself atop his hands, but he'd always known this part would be dicey. He might not survive.

What mattered most was destroying the paperwork that kept Hollander's people richer than they actually were while crushing the souls of people like Cutter to preserve the status quo.

But it would still be great to survive.

He was in the heart of a volcano as flames surrounded him.

And the smoke came heavy after a while, as all the fraudulent paper burned.

Soon, as the structure failed, the walls would probably fall in on him. He was tied to the chair; he couldn't run until it, and ideally, his bindings, burned.

After a while, he was no longer boiling.

The sensation of waiting to die became peaceful.

We did it. We did it, Boots. I know Dorothy's alive. They'll have to let her go now. Fire trucks will come. They'll let her go, and they'll tell her never to return, and she'll do it. And Khalif and Gord, they're okay too. Amenity's people are survivors. They'll help them. Hollander never found them. Boots, my god, they're like the Whos on Christmas. The presents were stolen, but those bastards keep singing.

Cutter was falling asleep from smoke with a smile.

Then he felt himself dragged … into open air, the backpack hood dragged off so his face could lie on the grass. His bindings were cut, one by one.

He stood up to see the clerk, Jason, standing in front of him.

"It's okay," the kid said. "She's already gone."

"Who?"

"Your girl. Dorothy."

Cutter stood beside the burning annex, his ghost truck blackening in its heart. He could hear sirens already. He had no idea what to say or do. He stood there nursing burns that would be agony later, his wrists chafed and his insides beaten to stew, his lungs sick with smoke.

For the first time in his life, nothing was remotely what it had ever seemed. Were there sides in this struggle? Was it even a struggle at all?

A flash caught his attention. Cutter looked to the fence, not far away.

He saw the trio of Gord, Khalif … and between them, both men supporting Dorothy. They'd even cut a hole in the fence already, holding it open for him because nobody, after this, could ever possibly care.

"Go on," Jason said. "But on one condition."

"Name it."

"When I find you again, I want to join you. To be one of you. I owe it to my Abuela. I owe it to her memory for what I did to help them. Because of …" He looked at the burning annex. "Of *this*. So if I help you, you have to promise that when I come to you, you'll help me, too."

Cutter nodded, dumbstruck. "You'll get in trouble. They'll know you let me go."

But the clerk only smiled and slowly shook his head.

"How could that happen? *You're not even here.*"

A city-sized prison with little oversight and a snitch economy is the worst place for an ex-cop. Especially one who is losing his mind. It's *Escape from New York* meets *The Matrix* in this fast-paced, heart-pounding SciFi thriller by best-selling authors Johnny B. Truant and Sean Platt.

Get Pattern Black Today

A Quick Favor...

If you enjoyed this book, please take a moment to write a short review on your favorite online bookstore so other readers can enjoy it, too.

Thanks so much!
  Sean & Johnny

About the Authors

Sean Platt is an entrepreneur and founder of Sterling & Stone, where he makes stories with his partners, Johnny B. Truant, and David W. Wright, and a family of storytellers.

Sean is the bestselling author of over 10 million words' worth of books, including the Yesterday's Gone and Invasion series. Sean is also co-author of the indie publishing cornerstone, Write. Publish. Repeat. and co-host of the Story Studio Podcast.

Originally from Long Beach, California, Sean now lives in Austin, Texas with his wife and two children. He has more than his share of nose.

~

Johnny B. Truant is co-owner of the Sterling & Stone Story Studio, an IP powerhouse focusing on books and adaptations for film and television. It's the best job in the world, and he spends his days creating cool stuff with partners Sean Platt and David W. Wright, as well as more than 20 gifted storytellers.

Johnny is the bestselling author of over 100 books under various pen names, including the Fat Vampire and Invasion series. On the nonfiction side, he's also co-author of the indie publishing mainstay Write. Publish. Repeat. and co-host of the weekly Story Studio Podcast.

Originally from Ohio, Johnny and his family now live in Austin, Texas, where he's finally surrounded by creative types as weird as he is.

www.ingramcontent.com/pod-product-compliance
Lightning Source LLC
Chambersburg PA
CBHW010543100726
47903CB00011B/3118